TALES

A SHORT STORY COLLECTION

Happy

Rifting!

Mil

Also by Miles Nelson

Riftmaster
Renegade

The Forge & The Flood

Tales from the Rift

A Short Story Collection

Miles Nelson

Elsewhen Press

Tales from the Rift
First published in Great Britain by Elsewhen Press, 2024
An imprint of Alnpete Limited

Elsewhen Press, PO Box 757, Dartford, Kent DA2 7TQ
www.elsewhen.press

British Library Cataloguing in Publication Data.
A catalogue record for this book is available from the British Library.

ISBN 978-1-915304-49-0 Print edition
ISBN 978-1-915304-59-9 eBook edition

Designed and formatted by Elsewhen Press

This book is a work of fiction. All names, characters, places, planets,
alien empires and events are either a product of the author's fertile
imagination or are used fictitiously. Any resemblance to actual
events, extra-terrestrial federations, worlds, academies, places or
people (living, dead, or rifting) is purely coincidental.

CONTENTS

v

LiKe FaTHer, LiKe son

Many years ago and many lightyears away, a family of five thrived. Toby is the youngest of three children born to cosmic travellers Oliver and Ari, and the most eager to please. But when each day presents new challenges, and every world new unknowns, danger can spring from unlikely places. When his eldest sister is injured, Toby joins his father on an expedition to find a new source of food. But Toby and Oliver have never seen eye to eye, and while on their own in the hostile wilderness, getting along may be the least of their worries. With the family fragmented, both father and son will need to listen, learn, and most importantly, understand.

"Aria, stop! It'll kill you!"

From where Toby was hidden high amongst the broad-leafed red foliage, he heard his father's voice cry out. His other parent stood below him, facing a towering creature which leered down at her. Behind Ari crouched his elder sister who stared, chest heaving, up at the terrible beast. Adeline's eyes were round with fear as she clutched at her arm, blood oozing out between her fingers.

On two great, broad feet the creature stood with segmented tail lashing. Stubby forearms poised stiff and threatening, flexing massive claws. A long, curling neck led to clacking mandibles like serrated daggers. Enormous, teardrop-shaped compound eyes kept the tiny family in view.

"And leave my daughter to be eaten?" Ari stood tall, wielding a silver dagger scarcely any larger than one of the beast's talons. "No!"

As Toby watched in horrified fascination, Ari paced, drawing its eye. When it struck, she came dancing in, swiping, streaking, cutting at the gaps in the beast's segmented rust-red hide. It leered, mandibles snapping shut on air as it lunged downwards. Ari dodged, then leaped forward.

Toby's heart missed a beat.

Grip tightening on the dagger, his parent plunged the weapon into one of the creature's eyes.

Ari twisted the blade until her opponent shrieked and writhed, thick purple blood gushing down her arm. She stepped back only when it lay still, yanking her silver knife from its skull. Toby remained where he was, protected by twisted stems of herbage and hidden by broad red leaves.

Wasting no time, Aria turned towards her daughter, kneeling in the iron-rich soil to tend her wound.

"Adeline, it's okay. You can move your hand, just let me see, alright?"

As soon as Adeline did so, blood gushed free, running in rivulets down her arm. She let out a choked sob.

"Okay, we've got this. Just... hold your arm above

your head, see? Yes, that's it! Good, now hold it there."

Toby was amazed by the sheer lack of panic in her voice, but he reminded himself that she'd seen worse, probably many times before. His own breaths still coming harsh and fast, Toby took his time removing himself from the tree. Finally, he dropped heavily onto the ground.

By the time he stepped out into the open, his father was standing beside Ari, his face reddened with rage and fear, blonde hair wild.

"Of all the stupid things I've seen–"

"Yes, yes, I know, *dear*. Toby, would you bring me my satchel?"

"Yes, Ari!"

Obediently, Toby scurried past his father, exchanging a nervous glance as he went. He could see the veins bulging on his father's temples and see his shoulders heaving.

Ari paid him no heed.

"Polly! Polly! Are you out there?!"

The undergrowth rustled. Toby's twin, blonde, freckled, and shivering, emerged.

"Aria–" Oliver said again, but he was soon interrupted.

"Go to the riverbank, grab me some mushrooms," Ari told her youngest daughter.

Polly's shoulders relaxed, and she looked visibly relieved.

"The ones with the spongy caps?"

Ari nodded, and Polly scampered away towards the distant sound of running water.

Before Ari could ask, Toby reached into the satchel and retrieved their waterskin, along with the linen strips that his parents used to tend wounds. There wasn't much left, but he offered them anyway. "Good lad!" Ari praised heartily. "Now, Oliver? Grab me a branch. No protests."

Leaving Adeline holding her arm up above her head, Ari yanked the dagger from the creature's head, the purple-stained metal gleaming dully. She cleansed it quickly under the water before washing the blood from her hands, wrists and forearms. Finally, she could clean Adeline's wound.

She snatched the branch from Oliver, and using the dagger, began to peel off strips of bark.

Quickly, Ari tied the strips of plant matter around Adeline's arm at the base of her shoulder, restricting the bloodflow. Finally, as Polly returned, she cleaned the edges of the wound and bound it with strips of linen.

Finally, Ari sat back, letting out a heavy sigh. Her stormy grey eyes met Adeline's, and she smiled slightly. "We're gonna be okay."

Adeline slowly lowered her arm, set her back against a lump of rotting vegetation, and sighed, eyelids drooping. She dropped her head onto her chest, panting, wild clusters of auburn hair falling around her shoulders.

Ari finally stood, and turned to Toby and Polly, offering them both a pat on the shoulder, and a nod. Finally, she looked up at Oliver.

"You're going to get yourself killed, picking fights like that. There's going to come one that you can't win," Toby's father growled. "And after all that effort, it's not even edible." Oliver looked with disgust at the trail of purplish blood-splatters that stained the red earth dark.

Ari's brows furrowed. "Oliver..." she said, her voice low with warning. "Our daughter is safe. Now is not the time."

Their gazes met, stormy grey against blue. Then Ari brushed past Oliver, red leather armour creaking gently as she stalked over to her satchel to check their supplies. Wavy red hair fell about her freckled face as she knelt, rifling through the satchel. "We're almost out of food. Let's worry about that before we worry about what's already done."

"Fine," Oliver said, through gritted teeth. "I'll go hunt something."

"Thank you."

Oliver turned, and swept from the clearing, bristling. Just before he left though, he glanced back.

"Toby! Come with me."

Toby looked up sharply, blinking with surprise.

Ari, too, raised her head, narrowing her eyes. "Are you sure that's a good idea?" she asked wearily.

"Leaves less for you to keep an eye on. Besides… It's time he learned to hunt. Especially if Adeline can't."

"Fair enough," Ari turned back to what she'd been doing without further questions. "I suppose I can trust *you* to be cautious."

She paused for a moment, before looking up once more.

"But if you dare come back here without him, I *will* douse you in sugar-root and feed you to the snappers. Understand?"

Oliver snorted, and turned away. "Try not to do anything stupid whilst we're gone."

Then he turned, leading Toby out of their tiny camp and into a dark, tunnel-like path of thickly entwined foliage. Before he left, Toby cast a glance back at his parent, who was watching him go. She offered him a parting nod, and he felt her eyes on his back all the way until the darkness finally swallowed them up.

***

Toby and Oliver journeyed in silence for quite some time, pushing forward into a darkness lit only by shafts of pale orange filtering through the tree canopy. Even in the half-light, it was as though the world was on fire; and Toby felt a small thrill of excitement and nervousness at the thought of finally being able to see more of this world. Creatures moved in the dark just beyond their sight, leaves rustling faintly. As Toby stepped ahead, a large, fluffy patch of burgundy moss darted out from under his foot on stubby legs. Others quickly followed, perching themselves on the stems of herbs before becoming still once more.

Realizing that he'd fallen behind, Toby hurried to catch up, and as he caught his breath, glanced back towards the now-motionless moss creatures.

"Can we eat those?" he asked.

"Poisonous," Oliver replied, without looking.

Toby walked on in silence for a time, looking around.

A group of small bipedal creatures the size of rats hopped across their path and away from them, waving feathered antennae and watching the humans pass.

"What about those?" Toby asked.

"You can try, but they taste foul," Oliver said. "…Although… Part of me wants to take one home for your mother."

Toby smiled slightly.

"Well then… what are we going to be hunting for?" he asked tentatively, as he shouldered through a curtain of leaves.

"There are only a few species with edible meats on this planet. We're going to be looking for something called a snuffler."

"What are those like?"

"They're about…" he stooped, and held his hand about three feet off the ground. "…this tall, with four dumpy little legs, and dark red skin. Their head juts out of the front of a big, round, fat body, and they have big claws and tusks to dig up roots. They can be dangerous if you're not careful, but they're so slow that you shouldn't find killing them too hard. Honestly, they are some of the stupidest looking aliens I've ever seen in my life…"

"Uh…" Toby fell silent for a moment.

"What is it?" Oliver broke the silence a moment later.

"Ari says that we shouldn't call them aliens," Toby offered tentatively. "After all, we're the strangers to their worlds."

Oliver huffed. "Yeah, well, your mother says a lot of things."

Toby wasn't sure why, but he felt a slight flare of indignation rise up inside of him. "That's because Ari knows how to survive better than anyone, even you," he pointed out.

His father grunted.

"…And you know she doesn't like being called

'mother', either," he added a moment later, in a low mutter.

Oliver must not have heard.

They trudged on in silence until the light filtering through the tree canopy had begun to dim. Only then did Oliver finally stop, and crouch down, scanning the soft earth. Toby approached on his left side, and followed his gaze, down to a few large, round tracks, with three distinct toes. Other than those, there were a few shallow grooves in the ground, following the path of the footprints.

"See the tracks?" Oliver said.

Toby nodded eagerly. "Yeah!"

"You should look closer. We can learn a lot from them," Oliver gestured to the large, three-toed prints in the moss. "These are the hind feet. Snufflers leave tracks in the same sort of pattern as we do." Oliver then gestured to the grooves. "And these are from its claws. Snufflers walk on hind feet with their claws curled under them. And sometimes, you can see them dragging their claws along the ground."

Oliver beckoned, and they crept alongside the tracks for some time. Toby squinted at the path ahead with narrow eyes, trying to see what his father saw.

"...That tends to mean they're injured." Standing up straight, Oliver kept going. "We'd better hurry along, if we want to be the ones to put it out of its misery!" he said cheerfully.

Toby followed, as quickly as he could.

By the time night fell, they still had not found the Snuffler.

The orange light of the sun faded, but their way was still lit by serpentine creatures, weaving through the air like ribbons. They glowed faintly pink as they spun in slow circles and danced around one another, pulsating softly.

It was only when red lights began to appear off the path that Oliver finally settled down to light a fire. As he did so, Toby looked around. The lights were vaguely flower-shaped, with four rounded points. They swayed gently in the dark. He was curious but knew better than to try and get a closer look.

A night on any world was dangerous, but curiosity was even more so.

Toby kept watch on the world around them as Oliver struck his knife to a shard of flint, producing a spark onto a small patch of moss. Finally, there was a hiss as the kindling took hold, and flared up into a flame of vibrant magenta. Toby's eyes opened wide, blinking in the sudden brightness. He looked around. A few broad-petaled flowers huddled close in the nearby vicinity, the tip of each petal glowing in the dark. All of them seemed drawn to the light, facing towards it. In the dark, he could not see their stems.

Toby blinked. *I could have sworn those weren't there earlier...*

Oliver picked up a stone and threw it at one of the flowers.

Each and every one snapped shut, revealing themselves to be the mouths of those small, fluffy moss-creatures.

They scurried away and were quickly lost in the darkness.

Toby settled down by the fireside, looking around as his father took up vigil. "You should get some sleep," Oliver said. "Tomorrow's going to be a long day."

Toby nodded and lay down, turning his back on his father and peering out into the darkness. As he struggled to sleep, he thought back to the last time he had been out on an expedition with his father alone. *Had* there been a last time? Between Oliver's desire for them to lead a cautious existence, and Ari's desire to ensure they *all* survived, the two of them clashed often, and did not always see eye to eye. Always they walked the knife edge out here, especially Ari.

But his other parent was patient and calm, somehow still finding fascination and joy in the unknown, whereas his father was...

Toby glanced up, and saw that Oliver was staring out into the dark beyond him, unblinking.

Toby shut his eyes once again. His father would not let him be hurt out here, he convinced himself. But still... Toby could not quite allow sleep to enfold him. He shivered, feeling eyes in the dark all the time, and missing the warmth of his sisters sleeping beside him.

Eventually, as pale moonlight began to filter through the tangle of undergrowth, Toby fell into an uneasy slumber.

***

"Dad?" Toby asked the next morning, as they picked their way through a tangle of herbage. He struggled to pretend he had slept well despite the creases under his eyes. Somewhere that morning they had lost the Snuffler's trail, and they both searched the area as they struggled to re-join it.

"Hm?" Oliver asked.

"Why did you bring me hunting with you?"

Oliver seemed surprised by the question. "You're my son," he said with a smile. "Of course I'm going to bring you hunting with me."

"But what about Polly? Why can't she come?"

"She's my daughter, Toby. She's different. She's too gentle to ever hurt anything out here. And besides... she has to help your mother."

"But what if I don't want to kill things either?"

"We're the men of the house, Toby. It's our job to."

Toby stopped, brows furrowing. "I didn't see you helping fight the thing that hurt Adeline."

Oliver turned towards him, a pained expression on his face. "Ari was the one who picked that fight, not me. She's not a fighter. Or... she shouldn't be, anyway."

"Well, she saved Adeline, and all of us, as well."

Oliver let out a sigh. "Well, there are times I wish she'd be more careful about it. After all, it's not just for her sake anymore."

Toby blinked. "What do you mean?"

Oliver's eyes widened. "You don't know?!"

"How would I know? Know what?" Toby asked, brows furrowing in frustration.

"She has your little brother or sister to think of, now," Oliver said through gritted teeth. "So if she's not careful…"

Toby's breath caught. He remembered, all of a sudden, the difficulty both parents had found in creating Ari's last outfits to fit her growing form, although he'd never seen her eat any more than the rest of them. The extra caution Oliver showed, and Ari's verbal jabs in response. And then, there was his father's near-constant need to be reassured, even though there were only so many ways Ari could say "I'm fine."

"When?" Toby asked, eyes wide with amazement.

"In 4 months, maybe three. If she keeps her wits about her until then."

Toby looked away, lips a tight line. "I'm just happy that Adeline is okay," he said.

Soon after that, they found traces of the snuffler's trail, and began to look around for evidence of its path. They seemed all but lost, until Toby drew his father's attention to a set of gouges on the stem of a towering plant.

"Well done," Oliver said, ruffling his son's hair until Toby's heart swelled with pride.

Together they followed the creature's trail up a sloping pathway, zigzagging wildly until they were well above the tree canopy. Finally, as the sun set beyond miles upon miles of forest, they settled down together in a sheltered alcove looking out over the horizon.

In the distance, a coil of smoke dissipated in the sky.

"That must be Ari and the others," Toby said, breathing a sigh of relief. "They don't seem nearly so far away from up here."

As the sun set, Oliver drew fragments of firewood and a small tangle of kindling from his satchel and sat down to light another fire. Toby watched him anxiously. Once, he opened his mouth as though to speak, but then stopped himself at the last moment.

Oliver looked up.

"What is it?"

Toby hesitated, looking away and out over the golden sky that was rapidly fading to deep maroon. "Do… you think we could wait on starting a fire for now?" he asked nervously. "Just for a few moments?"

"Why?" Oliver asked curiously.

"I just… haven't seen the stars from this world, yet," admitted Toby. "…This is the first time I've even seen the sky. I was hoping we could look at them… Just for one night."

"You like to look at the stars?"

Toby nodded.

"I know it can be dangerous without fire, but this plateau seems quite safe to me. I don't think anything will find us!"

Oliver hesitated. "Okay. We can wait until the stars come out."

They watched over the forest from above as the last slivers of sunlight faded into a blanket of deep purple. Then, one by one, the stars winked into view. Thousands upon thousands of them, more than Toby could ever hope to count.

"Is there anything you're hoping to see?" Oliver asked, finally.

Toby shrugged. "I… I was just wondering where we'll be going next."

Oliver followed his gaze, out across the vibrant starfield. He hesitated, then spoke.

"Has Ari taught you about the stars?"

Toby nodded. "She tried to teach me to navigate with them, once. But it's so hard to tell them apart, and they change whenever the Rift takes us to somewhere new. I…" Toby trailed off, and hesitated.

"What?" Oliver asked, gently.

"…I always try to look for the place you and Ari came from."

"Earth?" Oliver looked up in surprise. "Why?"

Toby shrugged, scratching the back of his head. "I just… can't help but wonder what it's like. I've never known anyone else like us in the universe, so… I can't imagine there being a whole planet full of us. Are there a lot of humans on earth?"

Oliver smiled slightly. "Hundreds of thousands," he said, somewhat absently. "Just like us, and not like us at all. Enough that we built huge cities and towns. Changed the course of rivers so that we could grow even more. We changed the very fabric of our world, and made it into something greater than just a lump of rock. We even went to the moon…"

"Which moon?" Toby asked.

"Earth has only one."

Toby's eyes widened. "Did you use the Rift?"

"No. They used metal and fire, and a lot of time and patience. Everything takes time, on Earth; it's not like it is out here, where time means nothing."

"Ari never told me about that," Toby said doubtfully.

"That's because it was after her time. Not mine, though."

"Oh…" Toby paused, looking up at the stars. "Did you ever meet Ari, back when you lived on Earth?"

Oliver hesitated. He looked down, and fingered the golden ring he wore on his left hand. He had worn it since before Toby was born, yet the boy had no idea of the planet it had come from, or what it meant.

Finally, he shook his head. "No. I didn't meet Ari until a long time after leaving Earth," he said. "I… had another family, before that."

"Was the ring a gift from them?" he asked.

Oliver chuckled. "In a way… yes."

"Do you ever miss them?"

Oliver looked up in surprise, before quickly glancing away. "I do. Of course I do, but…" Oliver reached out, resting a hand on his son's shoulder. "I have a new family now. And even if this life is difficult…" he looked towards Toby. "…I wouldn't change it for the universe."

Toby smiled slightly, relaxing. "What about Ari?"

Oliver looked out towards the distant tendril of smoke. "We argue a lot," he admitted. "But I wouldn't change her, either. I just…" He closed his eyes. "…I just worry about her."

"I…" Toby lowered his gaze. "I don't. Ari keeps us all

alive. There are times when I don't even think she needs us."

Oliver looked up at him, and Toby saw his own uncertainty mirrored in his father's eyes. "Of course she needs us. I just... don't think even she realises it."

Toby looked away, but inched slightly nearer until Oliver reached out an arm and brought him close. "It might not seem like it sometimes," Oliver murmured after a pause. "But I don't just worry about her."

Toby opened his mouth, but couldn't find the right words to answer him.

They watched the stars together until the moon reached its zenith, before finally settling down to sleep.

Just before he drifted off, though, Toby opened his mouth, and spoke in a tiny voice.

"Goodnight, dad."

***

Toby and Oliver awoke as soon as dawn touched the horizon, to a faint sprinkling of rain and a forest covered in glimmers of dew. They left camp quickly, and soon discovered a fresh set of tracks leading up the mountainside.

The pair followed them, hurrying after the snuffler up the mountain. Toby's heart pounded with excitement, his stomach growling with renewed hunger. The meagre rations they had lived on for the past few days had taken the edge off their hunger but never quite filled them. Now that they were so close, their bellies ached for something more.

They found the snuffler digging for roots at the base of a stand of foliage. As Oliver had said, it was large, and round, with two enormous tusks and large, teardrop-shaped eyes. Its head was thick, protruding straight out of its shoulders. The creature was well-equipped for absorbing impacts, but probably not much else. Enormous, orangish tusks dug up roots, and with its claws it burrowed into the earth. One forelimb hung limp and useless at its side.

"I'll creep up on its right side," Oliver whispered. "Its wound means it won't be able to fight back. Watch what I do, and watch closely."

Toby nodded.

The snuffler was so engrossed in its own mission that it didn't notice them until it was far too late. With a stick they had carved into a sharp point, Oliver crept up on the side of its wounded forelimb. Toby waited and watched with wide eyes and bated breath. But he needn't have worried. It fell, quickly and cleanly, with a single blow.

Then, after brief celebrations, Oliver slung the body across his shoulder and the two of them began the long journey back home. This time, they laughed and joked along the way.

***

They arrived shortly after dusk. The first thing Toby noticed was that Adeline was awake, her cheeks flushed and wound bound, and she seemed just fine. Although wobbling slightly, she stood to greet her father, and ruffle her younger brother's hair despite a giggled protest.

Ari stood from where she had been tending the fire, and for the first time, Toby noticed the exhaustion in her eyes as she swept over to offer Toby a hug and a kiss upon the brow. Oliver dumped the carcass on the ground beside them, and his parents took one another into a silent embrace.

As they stepped apart, Toby smiled. "You didn't get in any fights while we were gone, did you?"

Aria smiled, glancing back towards Adeline before winking. "Only with your sister," she chuckled.

Toby laughed but noticed that Oliver remained silent.

Ari looked up at her partner, brows creasing. "What's wrong?"

"I…" Oliver looked away, folding his arms. "I… it's just… You worry me, sometimes. You're reckless, and you're impulsive. You act first and think later. I just worry for you, and…" he glanced back towards her.

"…And for our family. I don't think I could do this alone, Ari."

Ari's gaze softened slightly. "I… I understand *that*, Oliver," she murmured. "Although… I know it might not seem like it sometimes. I'll try to be more careful from now on." Her gaze hardened slightly. "But if it comes to it, I can't promise I won't protect my family."

"That's all I can ask for."

Oliver pulled Ari into a tight embrace before offering her a whiskery kiss on the lips.

Finally, Oliver pulled away, glancing around at their small, gathered family, and offering a smile. "Well then… Who's hungry?"

Together, they hauled the carcass of the snuffler to the fireside, where they worked together to prepare the meat for cooking, harvesting whatever else they could for use in tools and leather.

Sometime later, the small family huddled together to eat, talking and laughing together for the first time in many days, and finally their worries were eased. The meat would last them at least another few days, perhaps longer if they preserved it properly.

Their current camp was getting too obvious, though; the scent of smoke and cooking spreading far, and likely to draw scavengers from the woods. Ari wanted to find somewhere else, somewhere she knew their little group wouldn't be found. "But where would we go…?" she wondered, aloud.

Toby's eyes shone. "I know a place!" he said, looking up at his father. "Right, dad?"

Oliver nodded. "Good thinking, Toby! I can lead us there."

And so they packed, gathering the few worldly possessions they owned. Finally, the three siblings stood before their parents.

Toby exchanged an excited glance with Polly, and her eyes sparkled back at him. Then he looked towards Adeline, her arm now in a makeshift sling.

Ari glanced over each of them in turn and nodded.

"Everyone ready?"

The three nodded in unison.

"Then let's go!"

They set off in a line on a familiar trail, leaving nothing more than a small, charred circle, and some scattered bones picked clean. Together, the family moved on, taking the first small step of their long journey.

And as they did, Toby felt his heart swell with excitement. The forest around them sang with noise, strange and beautiful. The sunlight flickered across shining red leaves and yellow tendrils, illuminating the forest trail ahead with dapples of shade.

As they walked, Toby briefly caught his father's eye, and the pair exchanged a silent smile.

THOSE THAT CAME FIRST

Bailey feels like it's been a lifetime since he left Earth. Now, light-years away, he looks to its future.

It has been 3 months since Bailey and the Riftmaster started travelling together. As the Riftmaster's apprentice, Bailey has learned how to survive the cruel ways of the Rift, overcoming impossible odds and hostile worlds. Now, though, the duo encounters something new; an alien city, long abandoned to the desert and the dust.

Bailey wonders what became of the people here and becomes wrapped up in its fate as he searches for answers. Still holding grimly onto hopes of returning to Earth, he seeks to bring something home; if not a solution, a warning.

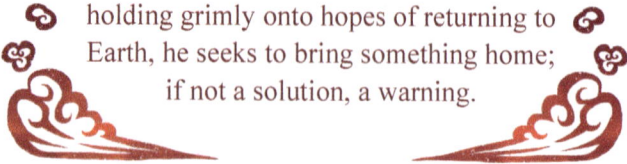

Bailey slunk after his mentor along a narrow mountain path. As his boots fell silently against a path that was worn smooth, he had the uneasy feeling that he wasn't the first to walk this way.

Against the ominous hum of the wind he considered his unbelievable, yet undeniable luck for what felt like the hundredth time. *Only he* could have ended up in this situation; kidnapped by the universe and dropped unceremoniously onto another planet. Ending up hopelessly lost in the infinite cosmos as he plunged haphazardly between dozens of hostile and terrifying new worlds.

And *only he* could somehow end up finding the only other human who had managed to survive a life like this.

Bailey froze as his mentor stopped ahead of him, cloaked figure still among jagged boulders that were streaked with roiling veins of copper, sickly-green.

For a moment, the Riftmaster listened to the shrill whine of the wind among the wreckage.

What have you heard?

Bailey's heart beat faster and he hunched low, knowing they could be seen by anything circling the wine-red sky. This world seemed, so far, as empty as it was cruel, but he still didn't trust it. He couldn't even tell if the skeletal grasses poking up around his feet were dead or alive, but at least they were something.

Seemingly satisfied, the Riftmaster let out a breath and then crouched. Bailey watched him test his fingertips on some grass, then pluck a clump from a vein of copper. Bailey slowly approached his mentor's back, looking questioningly over his shoulder.

"For kindling?" Bailey asked.

The Riftmaster looked up sharply, and Bailey flinched at the suddenness of it. His mentor blinked as though still surprised to find another human standing beside him.

The shadows beneath his eyes made his expression seem hollow in the half-light, skeletal despite his rounded cheeks. His explosion of freckles looked like blood splatters. Only the upright prickle of messy hair and the blink of ash-grey eyes betrayed any emotion.

21

"…Yes, that's right." The voice that answered him was high pitched and hoarse with disuse, but familiar. "Or… Maybe food. We can see when we find somewhere to hide."

Bailey nodded, shoulders relaxing as the Riftmaster turned away.

"…That said… this is no place for surprises, Rifthopper," his mentor added, eyebrows rising and a smile tugging at his cheek. "I almost took you for a carnivore."

Bailey glanced his way. Though the Riftmaster's voice was edged with humour, there was no laughter in his eyes. "I'm sorry, Riftmaster."

The Riftmaster's smile faded.

Bailey looked back the way they had come.

The long, jagged pathway looked no more inviting than it had any other time. But at least it was out of the wind.

Ahead of them, though, miles of barren plain sprawled, cruel gale billowing clouds of dust from the cracked, scorched earth.

Bailey swallowed, wishing that he was somewhere, anywhere else.

Especially home.

It felt like a lifetime since he'd last seen Earth. The memories alone made his heart ache in a way that still felt uncomfortably raw.

Lightyears away from everything he knew and loved, Bailey had spent the last three months being whisked from world to world at the cruel and unpredictable whim of the Rift.

Yet, that was nothing compared to the Riftmaster's five-thousand years.

In the half-light, his mentor's face was ashen, deep grey eyes leeched of their usual light. Red curls of uneven hair whipped his cheeks. His eyes held the same cool look that Bailey suddenly realised was anticipation. He squinted against the grit carried on the wind.

Against the faintest hint of sunlight, Bailey realised what his mentor was looking at. Rising sharply from clouds of sand stood a twisted tower. As the dust cleared, only for an instant, Bailey saw the horizon take shape, an uneven array of orderly lumps. It took a moment for him to realise what he was looking at, shivering in the fog. Miles of distance betrayed what he could only assume to be a city.

The Riftmaster stood, ready and poised to step out onto the wide, bare plain. But once they started walking, there would be no going back.

Bailey was tired. The wind whistled in his ears, and he wasn't ready to fight for every step.

"When do you want to stop to eat?"

The Riftmaster glanced back with an expression that was something between a smile and a grimace. He held out the clump of grass. Bailey didn't think it would be very nutritious. "I was hoping to find something a little more appetising than this."

"It... Isn't it poisonous?"

"Probably!" The Riftmaster smiled, an expression dusted with irony and tinged with the faintest hint of pride.

"Riftmaster... You're smiling as if that's a good thing!"

"Caution is always a good thing. If we don't find anything else, we can always eat what we have preserved."

"And then?"

"We press on. This city could be a good place to start. With any luck, it was built next to a water source."

Bailey grimaced, eyeing the waterskin his mentor always carried at his belt. It was almost half empty. "And if it isn't?"

"We can only try."

Bailey gritted his teeth and looked out across the plain, black hair whisking in the wind. It had grown, since he'd left Earth. "No food. Hardly any water. Burning sand, Hell-red skies and now the ruins of some long-dead civilization. I don't think this place could get any worse."

The Riftmaster scoffed faintly, wagging a finger at his

apprentice. "Rifthopper, the situation can always get worse. Don't tempt fate."

"You'll get us through it though, right?"

"I sure hope so!" The Riftmaster offered him a lopsided grin. "...But no promises."

They wandered between boulders that Bailey suddenly speculated might have been hewn into sharp angles by ancient tools. The Riftmaster's quiet footsteps seemed to barely skim the path. When the duo finally dropped onto level, cracked ground, the Riftmaster peered out towards the forlorn horizon and paced unsettlingly. In the relative shelter of the rocky mountainside, Bailey saw grit and sand whisking along the wide, flat plain. Sharp shards bounced across an empty void.

Silence reigned. By the time the Riftmaster finally stopped pacing, Bailey stared into the distance with resignation. On level ground he stood a head above his diminutive mentor, but the Riftmaster's pride made him feel about ten feet taller.

"I don't like this," Bailey said. "Have you ever seen a world like it before?"

"Unfortunately, yes."

Bailey expected his mentor to elaborate. But in this case, he seemed strangely distant. The Riftmaster pulled his fur cloak tighter around his shoulders, shielding himself from the wind. "We're going to have to walk in the open for a time. Do you still have your mask?"

"From the Mountain-dwellers?"

The Riftmaster nodded. "It'll protect us from the wind."

Bailey hesitated, fumbling at his belt from a moment. Finally he withdrew an ivory mask, shaded by a bright pink cowl. Its visage was modelled after the Mountain-dwellers, a goatlike species from a planet of bitter cold; back there, oxygen-rich herbs stashed in the muzzle had helped to prevent altitude sickness. Like the pink fur cloaks around each of their shoulders, it would help protect them from weather of almost any severity.

After an approving nod, the Riftmaster donned his own,

and crept out onto the open plain. Bailey hesitated, then followed. The wind hit him like a wall, and although they both braced against it, it was like wading through honey. Bailey saw the Riftmaster crouched low. Bailey copied the stance, his breaths deep and long.

The Riftmaster glanced back across his shoulder, checking Bailey's progress.

Sand hissed around them, and a hollow fluting sound rose distantly from the crumbled ruins.

"You know," his mentor yelled cheerfully. "I've heard instruments that sounded far worse than this wind. If I heard this playing in a Riftworld tavern, I'd probably dance to it."

Bailey looked up, trying to figure out if the Riftmaster was joking or not.

"From the sounds of it, you'd dance to anything," he called into the gale.

The Riftmaster laughed. "You're probably right!"

The distance to the city was further than they had thought. With no days or nights on this world, there was no way to estimate the time. Bailey's steps faltered as his muscles ached from straining against the wind. Since leaving Earth he had become stronger and fitter, but his endurance still had a long way to go.

The inside of Bailey's mask was coated with perspiration, small eye holes limiting his vision.

Finally, a shadow fell upon them. Bailey looked up to see the tower looming somewhere beyond the mist. But by this point, even the Riftmaster was flagging. Despite a short stature, his mentor's endurance was something to be admired. For every stride Bailey took, the Riftmaster made two. In the months they had known each other, Bailey had never seen his mentor tire.

Until now.

They struggled on until capes thrashed at their backs. Bailey breathed hard, focusing on the ground at his feet.

Step by step, he kept pushing onwards. But something felt wrong; somewhere ahead of him, the cracked earth ended. Beyond that, there was nothing.

Bailey took another step forward, straining to see.

No more than a metre ahead, the ground fell away into what might have been an abyssal moat.

Bailey looked up at the Riftmaster, but his gaze was on the ruins, his focus on how close they were to shelter, to safety.

"Riftmaster!"

Bailey lurched forward and grabbed his mentor's shoulder, yanking him back. The Riftmaster looked down over the edge into a terrifying drop.

They both stood for a moment, heavy cloaks shuddering, shoulders heaving. Bailey's mentor stared down into the dark that had very nearly ended him. And then he swallowed, looking up into Bailey's worried eyes, shadowed with exhaustion.

"Well done, Rifthopper."

"Are… are you alright?" Bailey asked, breathing heavily.

The Riftmaster gave the slightest nod. "I've almost died in far worse ways," he said, though his tone of voice belied his humour. "But this would have to be the most embarrassing."

"You can tell me about those later," Bailey said. "I… I don't think now is the time for a story."

"No, no. Probably not." His mentor's expression cheered abruptly. "On the bright side, I think we've found a water channel."

Bailey said nothing, breaths hot and thick and echoing within his mask.

"…Bailey?"

Bailey glanced down, abruptly realizing he still held the Riftmaster with a dead man's grip. Their gazes met, and the Riftmaster replied to his unspoken question with a slight nod. Slowly, he unhooked his fingers.

His life was worth the bruises.

"I just hope we can find a bridge soon."

The ruins loomed, tall and broad. The duo followed the dry canal along its snaking way, watching long-fallen structures pass. In some places a coating of black fuzz still covered the stone at the very bottom, where water must have flowed until quite recently. Finally, they found a narrow walkway across the canal, and entered the city in single file.

It was empty. Although Bailey had never really expected to find life here, his stomach still sank.

Some of the buildings had collapsed, looking like cracked eggshells in the dark; but most seemed built for this sort of weather, still standing stoically against the sandstorm. Rivulets of copper stuck out where stone had worn away. They examined ancient doorways in a weird procession of shapes and sizes. With each one, Bailey prepared to see someone watching them, hackles rising.

Then he deflated when there was nobody there.

Finally they emerged into a narrow walkway between still-standing buildings.

Bailey swallowed as he paused to peer under another empty arch. "Do you think we're really alone?" he asked. His voice felt painfully loud in the silence that was only broken by the keening wind.

The Riftmaster looked around tentatively. He shrugged. "I doubt it. If there's shelter to be found among the ruins, there will be something living in it."

Bailey didn't ask any more questions after that.

As they pressed deeper into the foreboding darkness, Bailey's breaths grew short and clipped. The Riftmaster's hand fell to the knife sheathed against his thigh.

Finally, he beckoned Bailey through a narrow stone archway into a building that might have housed someone far taller than themselves. It had taken him a long time to settle on this particular ruin. There was another entrance, a smaller one, that led to another narrow side-street, and the roof had begun to crumble but was mostly intact. There was no way they could be cornered here, and the smoke from their campfire could escape and disperse.

The Riftmaster assumed the duty of setting up camp; using their cloaks as curtains to hide the camp from prying eyes. He hummed along to the howl of the wind as he carefully arranged their possessions beside the meagre fire. His expression flickered in surprise when Bailey helped without being asked.

He took his mentor's knife carefully from his hand, and struck it against a flint bead his mentor slipped from one of his necklaces. As the spark caught hold of some dry grasses and flared into a greenish-hued flame, Bailey finally let out his breath in a heavy sigh.

Only then did he look around.

Rivulets of copper shone faintly in the firelight, marking the mortar joints between puzzle-like blocks of grey-brown stone. It gave the otherwise empty room vague implication of style.

Very little of the previous inhabitants seemed to remain. But Bailey felt their ghosts all around him.

As they took turns drinking from the waterskin, Bailey settled with his back to the wall, forlorn and exhausted but unable to sleep. Sharpening his knife with long, slow rasps, the Riftmaster watched him, but said nothing.

Finally, Bailey spoke. "I... never thought I'd see a place like this," he said.

The Riftmaster glanced up, blinked.

"Like what?"

"Like a city," he said. "Only... it's so dead, so empty."

The Riftmaster tilted his head. "I suppose it would be quite a shock. But, you've met sentient races before, like the Mountain-dwellers. You know they're out here."

"But this... this isn't a sentient race. This *was* a sentient race."

Bailey paused, opened his mouth, then closed it again. *I worried about this,* he wanted to say. *About change. Extinction. About my kind slowly killing the Earth.*

"I don't know what happened here, but it feels..." Bailey trailed off. He brought his knees up to his chest. *Too close to home.*

He rested his chin on one knee.

Bailey heard a rustle as his mentor shifted positions. His expression was sombre as he knelt at Bailey's side. "Don't cry," he said gently. "We need to preserve water."

Bailey looked up, opening his mouth to protest until he

saw the Riftmaster's expression. Then he sighed and said nothing.

"This is only one city. There's a big chance these people still live on, somewhere warmer and wetter."

Bailey slowly lowered his legs and looked away for a moment. "Riftmaster?" The tiredness in his eyes had returned. "…When you lived on Earth… did anyone ever worry about the planet? And what humanity was doing to it?"

"I don't recall. My memories from back then are… fuzzy."

"I'm sorry, I… forgot it had been so long."

The Riftmaster shrugged. "It's alright."

There was a long pause before the Riftmaster finally spoke, tone tentative. "…Remind me, Rifthopper. You decided it was easier to hold onto hope of going home one day, didn't you? So why not hope that your people might surprise you when you do?"

Bailey didn't answer, the silence chokingly thick. He stared into the greenish fire that crackled in the dark. *What if they already have? What if this is Earth?*

Finally, despite the tightness of his throat, he spoke. "You must be missing the stars."

The Riftmaster took a moment to consider, moving back to the fireside. He patted the space next to him. "I'm not sure if missing them is the right word," he said with a smile. "I know they're always there." He sheathed his knife and settled back, resting his weight on his palms.

Bailey shuffled over to his mentor, tawny skin sickly green in the firelight.

"But… I do feel quite lost without them. I like to know my place in the universe."

"Do you know the names of all the stars?" Bailey asked.

The Riftmaster shook his head. "I only remember a few from my time on Earth."

"Maybe you should start naming them yourself."

The Riftmaster grinned.

"I'll leave naming things to you. I have too many

memories, too many routes and foods and routines…
there's not enough space in my head for much else!"

"If you say so."

"Though…" The Riftmaster dropped his voice to a
conspiring murmur, and winked. "I do make up my own
constellations sometimes. I try to pick out the shapes of
creatures from different worlds."

"Aliens?"

"No. Not aliens." The Riftmaster smiled. "We're the
only aliens here."

"Oh… right." Bailey nodded, and flushed red. "…I
forgot about that. Sorry, Riftmaster."

The Riftmaster turned back to the fire, grey eyes
watching the flame flicker and dance. "How about you
get a bite to eat and some sleep? You look exhausted."

"Will you keep watch?"

"Of course. I don't trust this place any more than you
do." The Riftmaster peered out into the empty street.
"You'll have to come up with a dastardly name for this
place when we leave."

***

The Riftmaster shook themself awake from a shallow
slumber and found that the wind had ceased its fervent
whine. The first thing they noticed was a lingering pain in
their shoulder, bruises from Bailey's vice like grip.

The second thing they noticed was that something was
wrong. They blinked around at scattered possessions,
strange surroundings, and the fire that had since burned
down to ash. *It's not like me to fall asleep while on
watch.*

They blinked a few times, steadying their thoughts.
Bailey…?

The Riftmaster shook their head, staggering upright, and
lurched over to the curtained entrance of the small, round
dwelling. They couldn't see much of the street where it
wound around a labyrinth of small stone houses. Bailey was
nowhere to be seen. The Riftmaster backed further inside,

darted across the ashes, and looked out the other door.

They heard his footsteps before he appeared around a bend, hair dishevelled and face troubled.

"Bailey!" they hissed. "Why didn't you wake me?"

"S-sorry! I wasn't going far, and…" He hesitated, but only for a moment. "I thought it might injure your pride."

If there was one thing that the Riftmaster could say for the young man, it was that he wore his heart on his sleeve. Their shoulders relaxed.

"Waking up on watch duty injured it regardless!" they said, expression softening as they held the curtain aside. "…But that doesn't matter. Something's wrong. What's wrong?"

"I…" Bailey rubbed a bristly cheek, glancing away from them as he moved to the fireside. "I was wondering if you'd help me figure out what happened here," he finally said. "This building is empty. The others seem to be too." He paused. "There are no bodies. If the people left in a hurry or died, there would be something left behind. So what happened?"

The Riftmaster took a moment to consider. Between the clinging feeling of their parched throat and a low growl in their belly, they had more pressing concerns. "Survival should always be our first priority," they said. "The answer won't mean anything to us if we die trying to find it."

"Er, well," Bailey stammered. "It was just a silly thought–"

The Riftmaster held up a hand to silence him, shifting their legs into a more comfortable position as they settled at the fireside. "…But, when our waterskin is full and food stored, perhaps." They tipped their head slightly. "But, tell me something, Bailey. Why?"

"Wh… Why?"

"Many different alien tongues have some variation on 'curiosity killed the cat', and in a place like this… well. Why should we care?"

Bailey took a moment to think. "Well… what if the thing that drove them out is still here?" he asked tentatively. "This could be the only place for miles that has water and shelter. If it's... alive, it would have a reason to stay."

The Riftmaster's eyes gleamed. "Just the answer I was looking for," they praised. "Even if I know you're lying."

Bailey looked away as they stood, stretched, and began to pack. Finally they stood by the entrance, holding the curtain aside.

"Come, then! We'd best get foraging and watering out of the way if we're going to beat the weather. I'd like to find a place for my garden, too."

Bailey hesitated, looking at them questioningly.

"Perhaps you should take the lead."

Bailey's eyes widened, hair standing on end. "In a place like this!? Can't you teach me somewhere a bit less..." he hesitated. "...Hostile? Hot? Dead?!"

"This life we lead won't often give us a choice, Rifthopper." They grinned at his stricken expression. "Don't worry. I won't let you get us killed."

"Where should I take us?"

"Where do you think we'll find the best chance of surviving?"

Bailey thought for a moment. "The canal was still damp. We should try and find the source."

The Riftmaster nodded approvingly.

Soon after, the duo padded out of their shelter and headed into the labyrinth, leaving only the ruins of a fire behind. To help learn the terrain, the Riftmaster gathered the ashes, and made scuffs on the tumbled walls to mark their path.

Without the crushing weight of the wind, the Riftmaster felt light and agile, clambering over tumbled walls and up onto the sloping domes of buildings to look out across the cityscape. From here, it seemed to go on forever; the great, tall tower marking its centre and judging them from the clouds.

It didn't take long to discover small, flat creatures spread out on the stones, taking advantage of the thin sunlight and the break in the wind. Wavering feelers appeared to filter nourishment from the dust, their bodies mottled brown for camouflage. Stuck in place and unprepared for predation, the most difficult part was prying one from the roofs of the dwellings.

The Riftmaster checked for a mouth and found the creature's underside clung to their palm like gecko feet. It didn't *seem* poisonous, but they would need water to know for sure.

Their journey continued its tedious and winding route, picking around small dwellings and rubble. In the meantime, the Riftmaster realised that the creatures would cling to almost anything.

Bailey's expression was severe as he stalked ahead, fists clenched, and pace determined.

The Riftmaster waited until there were a few metres of distance between them, and then hurled an unfortunate creature. It stuck fast to the back of Bailey's cloak. They stifled a snort, peeling another from its perch. Unused to having time to spare, they turned it into a game. Time would tell how many they could stick to their apprentice without him noticing.

Transporting the creatures would be a lot easier from that point on.

Bailey was not amused when he finally noticed the extra weight and discovered the host of passengers clinging to his back, but the Riftmaster cackled like a hyena.

"Think of it as another lesson for you, Rifthopper – always watch your back!"

After a while, Bailey finally caved in and allowed himself a tiny smile.

Finally the novelty wore off.

When they reached the edge of the ruins, their path joined the canal. As yesterday, though, the waterway was too deep to jump into, and its sides were smooth with the waterflow. The creatures that Bailey had dubbed 'slapjacks' had taken residence there, swollen round with water and algae.

They pressed on, hoping that the still-damp canal

would eventually lead them to its source. But the trek was long. Before they reached its end, they could stretch their water supply no further, and their water pouch finally ran dry.

"Before long, we might need to chance a leap," Bailey said, sounding resigned.

"Or, we could cut up our cloaks and make a rope ladder," his mentor pointed out.

"But then, what if the next world is cold?"

"We'll just have to deal with that when we get there." Although their voice was even, the Riftmaster was about as eager at the prospect as he was. "We… won't always have the luxury of planning ahead. Sometimes you need to make sacrifices in the moment."

Sometime after, the duo reached another narrow crossing that spanned the dry canal. Keeping low, they darted across.

Barren wasteland lay on the other side; but at least from here they could see foul weather approaching.

As they followed the waterway around the boundary of the city, they found themselves passing over a low, crumbled wall that enclosed a wide area of the plain. Bailey spotted a shelter that looked like an upturned bag, rumpled but round. Unlike the rest, boulders scattered this section of wide-open plain.

Here, the canal's sheer side became a gentle slope.

"I think this must have been a corral for animals," Bailey said. "The canal has a bank so they could drink."

The Riftmaster beamed. "It must have been!"

Curiously, Bailey moved towards the shelter, while the Riftmaster trotted towards the waterway's sloping bank. A few paces later, they were called back. "Riftmaster? You're going to want to look at this."

The Riftmaster approached with a measure of caution.

Beside Bailey was a jagged boulder, but as they drew nearer, the texture became smooth and shiny, and they could pick out different segments – the foremost of which possessed two symmetrical holes. At some point, the realization hit them that this was the huddled husk of some great creature. Six-limbed, smooth, and streamlined, the wind curled over it even now. It was curled with its back to the wind, its inside hollow with age. The Riftmaster lifted their head, peering around them at other boulders. The more they looked, the more they seemed to see; beasts of burden that had lived out their days in a dried-out corral.

Or…

"They must have died of old age," the Riftmaster said. "if the water had receded, they could have entered the canal and escaped."

"I'm not so sure," Bailey said, gravely. "Some of them have wounds."

With his boot, he shifted what the Riftmaster had taken to be a part of the dead thing. Another exoskull, narrower and with two immense curving horns, turned over. Sand poured from its empty eye sockets. Bailey knelt and pulled a rusted copper blade from beside it, leather straps breaking away from the body beneath the sand.

Bailey dropped the blade at his feet.

They had found the city's inhabitants.

"Bailey…? We should move on."

Bailey seemed torn, hesitating. Something wrestled with the ache for water that they knew he needed just as much. They knew that thirst would soon win out, but they felt concern growing. Was this answer so important that he would risk death to find it?

"…Bailey."

It seemed the encouragement was enough.

"Let's keep on moving," he said finally. "We need to find water."

He turned his back on the shelter and the fallen creatures, although his mentor's gaze lingered for a moment longer, thoughtful.

"Do you think we could use these?"

Bailey paused, looking hesitant. "What for?"

"Depends what we need. It seems quite sturdy, but we don't need more armour or souvenirs."

A strip of leather could make this into a fine shield,

they thought. But shields were cumbersome, and not always as useful as they seemed. They eyed their apprentice, thoughtful.

Catching their gaze, Bailey's expression matched theirs. "Perhaps we could use part of the exoskeleton for a cooking pot?"

"Yes, could be! Let's see!"

The shell was hard, but slightly bendy. Curved, and cool to the touch. Years lying in the sand had failed to wear it down, but it was shockingly light. The Riftmaster weighed it for a second in their hands before tucking it under an arm.

They waited as Bailey trotted ahead of them, and then hurried down into the canal, sliding only briefly on a film of algae beneath their feet. Stagnating puddles surrounded them. The Riftmaster eased a swollen creature from the rock face with their knife and offered it to Bailey. He held it for a moment, looking more than a little bit uncomfortable.

The Riftmaster set down their satchel and brought out three clay bowls, and three small pouches. They beckoned him over. "Settle by me. I'll take the lead for now."

The Riftmaster took a small pinch of blue flower petals from the first pouch, and showed him how to grind it down into a fine powder with the pommel of their knife. Then, the Riftmaster made a small puncture wound in the creature's side, and warm water flowed free. They let a little bit drip into the bowl, and thought for just a moment before speaking.

"The blue herbs detect acidity and alkali," the Riftmaster explained, their expression growing distant. "A little bit of either is okay, but you don't want to drink anything that will burn. If it fizzes, turns red or dark blue, avoid it like the plague. If it turns purple, then it may be some form of venom. But you'll need the red herbs to know for sure."

As they spoke, the Riftmaster's eyes lit up.

They had repeated this lesson many, many times; both for themself and others. The Riftmaster's expression grew slightly wistful. They could recite it almost without thinking. And they knew that for Bailey's sake, they'd need to repeat it many more times.

But their patience was limitless.

Bailey nodded slightly, but they gave him another moment to let the information sink in. Then they sloshed the water around to stir it.

"What do you think?"

"Er... looks good to me? It's slightly blue, but not dark."

The Riftmaster nodded approvingly.

For the red herbs, they allowed him to grind the powder and offered a similar explanation.

"What do you think, Rifthopper?"

"Hm? Oh, it seems clean, right?"

"So far, yes! But you mustn't skip the final step. This one is for dissolved minerals. Listen for the fizz, this time. It's a good thing."

From the last pouch they removed a black leaf. They crumbled it in their palm and showed it to him before adding it to the final bowl.

It fizzed lightly on contact, and then their shoulders relaxed.

"Did you get all that?"

Bailey nodded.

"Good. Now how about you test our dinner?"

Now that they knew it was safe, they lifted their knife and slit open the creature.

Clean, filtered water flowed free; they drank it straight from the source, much to Bailey's horror, and their amusement. There wasn't much, but for now it would be enough.

Wiping a smear from the corner of their mouth, the Riftmaster offered him the wriggling creature.

***

The new cooking pot worked like a charm, and as their broth boiled, Bailey helped to filter water from stagnating pools and muddied hollows.

The Riftmaster set a covering of leather across the cooking pot, letting the condensation slowly fill the waterskin over time. He kept an eye on the sky as the wind began to echo in low moans over the fallen city. While their start on this planet had been shaky, Bailey found himself slowly relaxing now that the waterskin and bellies were full.

It was his turn to keep watch while, after a half-hearted protest, the Riftmaster fitfully slept, tossing and turning by the fireside. In the quiet, that feeling of discomfort came creeping back. He knew that he needed to find answers before the Rift whisked them away and the opportunity was gone, forever.

Like an eternal watcher, the tower loomed, the wind howling about its curves.

He could see it in his mind's eye, like bubbles blown in stone, or a thousand little domed clay houses stacked haphazardly on top of each other, an eldritch palace fit for an alien king.

Who had lived there, and what had happened to them?

Bailey didn't know if he would ever find out, but he knew he would have to try. The Riftmaster wouldn't understand; he had been away too long. Although Bailey liked to think that his mentor cared about the planets he visited, he didn't think the Riftmaster liked to dwell on what might have been.

The Riftmaster lived in the now, and never looked back. The name that he'd used on Earth was useless, long forgotten by all but him. Instead, he favoured a name that could be spoken in any tongue. With a small clench of guilt, Bailey remembered the joy flitting across his face as he found fascination in life and nature. But he never spared a moment for those long gone. Just as leaving a world severed his connection to it, death was an end.

Skulls were just skulls to him; bones just tools to be used. He had made Bailey's armour from the hide of a fellow Rifter, as he told Bailey stories of its homeworld with wonder and reverence.

The Riftmaster didn't know what came after death and

38

had made it clear that he didn't plan on finding out.

But Bailey wanted to know what had happened here. Only then, he felt, could this place finally put its ghosts to rest.

Even so, the Riftmaster's question bothered him, itching in the back of his brain like a flea. Why did he care? He had never been here before, and never known its creatures or its people. It was nothing like Earth, he told himself, or anything else he had ever known.

But what if the inhabitants here shared Earth's fate? What if there was something he could learn, something he could do?

Even if Bailey never made it back, he knew he had to try.

Bailey rested his chin on his knees and waited for his mentor to awake, brows knotted and knuckles clenched around his knees.

When the fire had burned down to ash, the Riftmaster finally cracked open his eyes, and stretched. Bailey was on his feet before he'd sat upright, their belongings already packed. The amusement in the Riftmaster's eyes died as he saw the expression on Bailey's face. He quickly stood.

The Riftmaster didn't know what he was looking for. He didn't know why Bailey cared. But he would follow without question.

***

Bailey led the way at a speedy trot along the canal, the same way that they had plodded the night before. There had been a substantial argument before Bailey finally conceded that it would be best to keep following the waterway.

At first, Bailey wanted to go back the way they had come, returning to the ruins and heading for the bulbous tower. But the Riftmaster was unwilling to forego stable food and water supplies. Besides, he reasoned, when they reached the natural end of the canal, they could make camp and continue the search from there.

Much to Bailey's relief, the towering walls did not remain impassable forever. The further they walked, the wider and shallower the waterway became. Deposits of bricks and broken debris made Bailey confident that it would be possible to climb back out. Finally, they reached a dead end, where an ancient dam still leaked the tiniest trickle onto the ground. Although the drainage valves looked to have been out of use for many, many years, a few leaks had sprung from shallow cracks near the very bottom. Thinking of the stagnant pools, Bailey didn't think much water would remain on the other side.

The Riftmaster slapped a creature onto one of the cracks. Somehow, it succeeded in blocking the flow.

"There – fixed," he joked with a lopsided grin.

Bailey couldn't resist a smile. His heart wasn't in it, but he knew the Riftmaster was only trying to help. "Those creatures swell up when there is water – but we keep finding them on the roofs! Do you think the dam might have burst?"

The Riftmaster looked thoughtful. "I think it's more likely they store water when it rains and save it for the drier months. Creatures that live in the water permanently would have dried out a long time ago. Plus, the city would bear signs – there are no algae or weeds sprouting, or sedimentary deposits. It's as though the people here…"

"…just vanished." Bailey finished.

The Riftmaster nodded. He glanced around. It was relatively sheltered here, with access to clean water and food. Then he looked back at Bailey questioningly.

No – Bailey told himself, with a sudden surge of triumph. *Not a question, a test.*

"This place is too enclosed to make camp. If we were attacked here, there'd be no way for us to get out."

"So…?"

"Let's… ah… how about we do some gardening?"

The Riftmaster's eyes sparkled. He opened up his satchel and held out one of his herb pouches.

"Let's bring some life back to this place."

The soil was thin, but enough. They worked together to till a small section of hardened sediment and bury the seeds.

In a few days, the seeds would burst into small blue flowers, which in turn would make the soil safe for the rest.

When they had finished, the Riftmaster looked around at the shallow walls of the canal. He padded over to a wall on the city-side, but the nearest handhold was just out of his reach. "Bailey? A hand?"

Bailey hurried over to assist him, cupping his hands. The Riftmaster stepped into his palms and a moment later, was over the edge. Soon, Bailey was being hoisted up as well, trying to hide his surprise at the strength packed into his mentor's stocky body.

Soon, the pair sat together beside the dry canal, looking at what might have once been a wide, slow-moving pool. By following the waterway, they had found their way into the very centre of the city. Bailey looked up, found the bulbous tower stretching above them – and realised that, despite changing direction, the canal had led precisely where they wanted to be.

They could look out to see the channel threading through the ruins, and the tumble of tiny dwellings seemed to go on forever. A billowing sandstorm crept across the distant plain.

Bailey allowed a moment to admire the view. Then he turned away.

He set a slow pace, wandering cautiously around the perimeter of the tower, and the homes sprawling from its base.

Although time moved slowly on, this world seemed trapped in perpetual stasis. The sun did not rise or set. It just hung there, looming like a broken clock face. Bailey lost track of how long he walked.

He did not enter the tower at first; he wanted to look inside the smaller buildings, almost exactly the same as those on the outskirts.

Here, Bailey found the first signs of unrest.

Initially, he found belongings, packed to go. Satchels, saddlebags, pouches crammed with preserved meats and long-withered leaves. The still, dry air had kept it all dusty but unchanged. The Riftmaster eyed the weathered bags with some interest.

"We could take one?" he suggested. "You've been needing a satchel."

"Riftmaster…" Bailey sighed and shook his head. "Not this time."

The Riftmaster shrugged, expression downcast. "They would probably be brittle with age, anyway."

Though many buildings were empty, the closer to the tower they drew, the more evidence of life Bailey found. Evidence of beings that had once tried to escape but were unable to.

In the next, a forlorn exoskeleton lay crumpled next to its belongings. Bailey slowly and painstakingly looked through them, hoping to find some indication of what they were fleeing from. Yet the artefacts, which must have meant so much to those long dead, meant nothing to him.

Finally he sighed, shook his head, and stormed out.

The Riftmaster watched him from some distance away. His expression was unreadable, and he said nothing as Bailey moved on to the next crumbling ruin.

He dug into a leather satchel and finally drew out a scrap of chewed, dusty red linen. Painstakingly, he unfurled the tattered fabric. Strange, scattered markings might have been a form of writing, once. After spending some time trying to decipher it and a mystified shrug from the Riftmaster, Bailey returned it to the pile, and pulled out another. This one looked like an art piece, at first; the red dyeing was fainter, older, with blotches of watery copper-green. It was just as meaningless; but even so he squinted at the stylised knots of lines and pathways. Eventually, he realised that it was a map. Markings Bailey had thought were glyphs seemed to represent the city buildings. He spotted the canal looped around the city with water spilling out onto a green-dyed plain.

The corral was marked with tiny symbols of six-legged beasts.

The buildings stood in joyous disarray, clearly marking this city, and one or two others as well. He could see the mountains from where he and the Riftmaster had come, their path marked with copper paint, and the dammed lake set into a volcanic crater above the city, perfectly round. The path continued along the plain to the next city, then the next, before finally looping back in a perfect circle.

…But there was no tower drawn on the map.

Bailey looked out of the rounded doorway, and saw it looming over them, an amalgamation of the city buildings below. What could possibly lie inside?

The Riftmaster popped his head into the building from where he kept watch. Seeing the fabric, he tipped his head. "Find what you were looking for?"

Bailey sighed and shook his head. "Only more questions," he said, hauling himself to his feet and folding up the map. *I'll take nothing else, but the Riftmaster will appreciate this.* His knees clicked, stiff from kneeling.

Finally he made his way out into the open. He wound his way between buildings, reminded himself what he had found in each one.

Two bodies, packed belongings. Letters. A… waterskin, I think, and leather ropes.

Empty.

A sleeping roll on the floor of that one. One small bag, empty except scraps of linen and… some kind of pen?

A copper blade in here, and copper plates. No bags.

Same for that one. And that… and that.

The homes were sparsely decorated, except for the shimmering mortar joints. It lent them an air of impermanence, although they had clearly been built to withstand the sandstorms and the wind.

Finally, Bailey found himself standing before a great arched entranceway, leading into a huge circular hall. He looked up and saw the tower directly above him.

He wasn't sure why, but his heart beat faster.

I may find nothing within, he reminded himself. *So why does it feel like all my efforts have been leading to this?*

Bailey turned away and found himself trapped by the Riftmaster's concerned gaze. "You don't need to do this, you know," his mentor said gently.

Bailey shook himself and stepped over the threshold.

The tower hall immediately felt different. Intricate patterns of copper made it feel immediately opulent. Exoskeletons draped in chainmail lay dutifully where they had fallen either side of an arched doorway. The Riftmaster stepped over the remains without looking twice, stopping only to pick up a chainmail shawl.

"Riftmaster!" Bailey hissed. "Put that down!"

The Riftmaster's brows raised and he glanced down. "They don't need it anymore."

"Still!"

The Riftmaster breathed out a small sigh, then dropped the garment on the ground with a clink. "It would be too noisy for our purposes, anyway." He mumbled, and moved on.

The Riftmaster said nothing as Bailey searched, but peered into dark corners and corridors, always keeping a hand on the pommel of his knife.

Bailey padded the length of the room, looking for traces. His feet whisked up curls of dust, and revealed the shimmer of polished stone, likely brought in from somewhere else.

This hall at least had furniture, strangely rounded like everything else and gilded with copper. In one room he found a hole in the ground that might have once been filled with water from the canal, although the contraption attached to it was as alien as anything else.

A fountain, perhaps? Or... was this a kitchen of some kind?

Either way, the permanent fixtures were something new; Bailey had noted that every building except the tower was completely empty of furniture.

In any case, the people in this tower seem to have had running water.

There was not much else he could glean here.

Bailey slowly made his way through an arch and onto a tightly curving spiral of stone. The ceiling above stretched off into abyssal darkness lit faintly by shafts of red light.

"Bailey!"

He glanced back.

"We should go. I don't want to get stuck or cornered!"

"Stay here if you like," Bailey said. "I'll only be a moment."

Up, and up, and up the pathway wound. Bailey's footsteps echoed and soon he was gasping, his hair growing shiny with sweat. The pathway became narrower, its curves tighter, and he glanced down to see the ground dozens of metres below. Without a barrier between him and the fall, he gulped back the vertigo and forced himself not to look down again. But still he pressed on, with the Riftmaster walking closely behind him, brows knotted. Finally, an opening loomed ahead.

Bailey stepped out and into an empty room, decorated with copper tapestries of the city.

A single exoskeleton slumped beneath a window arch, drapes of blue-dyed linen threaded with copper beads.

Bailey stepped up beside the ancient remains and looked out to the distance. He saw nothing but the empty horizon, clouds creeping across the sky.

"There's... nothing here," Bailey said, the disappointment in his voice tangible. "Perhaps we should try looking somewhere else."

"Bailey..." the Riftmaster said gently. "Maybe it's time to stop. You'll never know the full truth."

Bailey turned to face his mentor. "But... If I don't, who will?"

"Bailey... This isn't your world."

"If you don't care about this, why did you come with me?" A sharp jab of indignance made Bailey's voice shrill. It startled him.

The Riftmaster's expression clouded. "I might not care about finding the answers," he said as he moved towards

Bailey's side, voice gentling. "But I care that you're hurting yourself trying to find them." The Riftmaster didn't look at him, watching the sandstorm slowly drift by. "I wouldn't be here if I didn't."

Bailey opened his mouth to speak, but no sound came out. He swallowed, and suddenly felt his heart tighten. "What if this is Earth?" he said, voice small. "You said that time is… fluid, out here, in the Rift."

"It's not Earth, Bailey. You've seen the skeletons."

"But Earth could become this, one day."

The Riftmaster said nothing. He looked up, and just for a moment, their eyes met.

Bailey swallowed and clamped his eyes shut. "…This place feels like home again, and not in a good way." He opened them again, gazing though tear-blurred vision out at the deep red horizon. "This planet… it's everything I was afraid of. Hot, and deserted, its people dead and skies cloudy with dust." He glanced down at the slumped, linen-draped exoskeleton beside him. "…But no-one important would do anything about it. I remember being one of thousands of voices clamouring to be heard, but no-one listening. And now that I'm gone…"

"You're just one person, Bailey… don't think of that responsibility as wholly yours."

Bailey looked down, tears shimmering on his cheeks. "I tried picking rubbish from the beach, but more would turn up the next day. The weather was getting nicer, but that's because the world was getting hotter. Soon, it will be like this." Bailey let out a deep breath. "Even if I do make it back to earth, what if I'm too late?"

"Bailey… You can try as hard as you want – but the weight of an entire planet is too much for one person to carry. Sometimes, what you're doing just won't be enough. And… That's okay." The Riftmaster sighed. "Some people back on earth would call me callous, but sometimes you need to be selfish. Take care of yourself first. Do you understand?"

"Riftmaster…"

The Riftmaster reached up and, after a moment's

hesitation, patted his apprentice's arm. "All that matters now is that you're alive, and that you're still taking the time to care. Sometimes, that's enough." He looked out again over the labyrinth of stone, the winding pathways that were so small from up here, like insect tracks in the dirt.

There was a momentary pause.

"For now, just look at this place, Rifthopper. Look at the view! If nothing else, at least you'll have a story to tell your apprentice, one day."

They glanced each other's way for a moment, before the Riftmaster looked back out over the city.

Bailey looked exhausted. He spoke as if he didn't quite believe his own words. "That... that's true." But as the light fell on his face, hope glittered in his brown eyes. A long silence reigned between them. "Riftmaster?"

"Mm-hm?"

"I'm... sorry I said you didn't care."

"That's okay, I... understand. I... I've been alone a long time. I forget that not everyone thinks like I do."

Bailey dipped his head. "...How about we head back to camp? We can gather food, harvest our herbs, and then..." he glanced out to the horizon. "...There were other cities on the map. Perhaps the others will have more for us."

The Riftmaster smiled.

"Sounds like a plan. We don't want to outstay our welcome."

The Riftmaster stepped aside to give him room to move. As they took their places side by side, Bailey noticed the Riftmaster's shoulders relax, and he looked happy at the opportunity to get back to their usual routine. "With any luck, the Rift will take us to somewhere prettier, next time," he said.

Bailey nodded, glancing at his mentor out of the corner of his eye. Before stepping onto the twisting walkway, he felt a flicker of bemusement.

I've told you about my life, about Earth. You know everything right down to my deepest fears. I have no secrets – but after all these months, I feel like I don't know a thing about you. Not your Earth name, not your history – not even the name of your last apprentice.

Sensing Bailey's stare, his mentor looked up curiously. "What?"

Bailey let out a breath. "It's nothing," he said with a small smile.

After a moment's hesitation, the Riftmaster smiled back. The expression seemed to hide nothing away.

You don't need to tell me anything, Bailey finally decided. *As long as you keep us both alive, I suppose I don't have a choice but to trust you.*

Bailey shook his head to dispel the thoughts and stepped out into the lead. But as he did so, the Riftmaster let out a stifled snort, and Bailey realised that a single hapless creature still clung to the back of his cloak.

War Dance

In the deep forests of another world, an unexpected meeting will sow the seeds of change.

The Valis are odd creatures, diminutive and weasel-like. They follow unchanging rhythms beneath the canopy of an ever-changing rainforest. As intelligent as the people of our world, Valis society has one key difference; they speak to one another by changing the colour of their skin. The foragers of Valis hives speak a complex and silent language, creating an intricate web of friends and family. The Queens, stowed away, have nothing.

All except for the Rogue Queen.

Valis legends tell of ancient Queens escaping the confines of their Hives, and this one happily takes the mantle when she leaves for the open wild. Far from home, she runs into another; a Forager who, for the first time, sees the other side of the coin. First, though, both have scores to settle… And when words aren't enough, the Valis have another solution: the War Dance.

There was a faint rustle as something passed among red-tinged ferns. Upon being touched, leaves withdrew, folding back into the tiniest bud. A path was cleaved through undergrowth which, after a while, gradually unfurled into a thick blanket once more, reaching up towards watery sunlight.

Something small shimmered faintly as it was uncovered, then quick as a flash, disappeared into more ferns. It nimbly skirted roots and hidden crevasses, weaving around boulders and over trees. A flash of scales disappeared briefly into a hole in the earth. Moments later, it reappeared as the creature scrambled out of a crack and climbed vertically onto a root that arched over a foraging trail. Then it melted back into nature, scales matching the faded purple of the wood. If it hadn't moved, the tiny being may have been a part of the root.

From there, the Rogue Queen observed her kingdom. Lavender-coloured eyes shone, catlike.

She had not expected to get lost.

Her scaled body shone in the faint sunlight, glistening with dew. A long row of spines quivered against her back. The tip of a segmented tail twitched nervously in the dark, barb shimmering wickedly; exposed like this, she needed to be prepared for anything. Although the colour of her scales melded perfectly with the dark and the wood, a distinct white cloud began creeping into the edges of her narrow silhouette.

This world was beautiful, new, and just for a moment, frightening. The rainforest was bigger and denser than she could ever have imagined possible, every tree soared like a vast pillar beyond her sight. The flowers were so much brighter than the Foragers had said, and she bathed in their neon glow, her scales reflecting the colours of their shine.

She had seen a flower only once; a small, pale offering she had requested from a forager long ago. It had quickly wilted into grey and disappeared.

Now, shining bright, their gleam reflecting in the colours of her scales, the Rogue Queen found the flowers were a hindrance. They made the simple act of camouflage deceptively complex.

For a moment she wondered if she regretted her venture into the unknown. But then she reminded herself what she had left behind.

Until now, she had known only the brown walls of the Valis Hive and the shades of dull boredom and contentment. Now she knew colour; more colours than she could ever have imagined. Beauty, and fear too.

Before she took her leave, the Elder Queen had offered advice and direction; painting intricate memories and simple maps onto her fading scales.

But the forest never stood still. The Elder showed the Rogue a different world than what could be seen today. Here there were different caves, different creatures, different trees. Saplings that had once clung to the roots of their parents had since crushed their aging trunks or ventured away to seek better soil. Those roaming trees now stood tall atop shattered terrain that their own roots had heaved from the earth.

The Elder Queen alone had lived long enough to see these worldly shifts, and she was huddled away in some dark and cosy corner of the Hive, and had been for a long, long time.

Nature had moved on, following the pattern of the light and bending the very earth to their whim.

The Rogue Queen watched sunshine filter down through the jagged tree canopy, casting mottled fragments down onto the forest floor. Deep violet foliage lent this place an ominous air, lit only by the neon rainbow of a thousand blooming flowers. Colourful, lizardlike creatures burst from tree to tree in great leaps, startled by something among the treetops. In the centre of the clearing, two trees, competing for the best ground, had wrapped roots around one another, and battled in silent stasis. The terrain beneath them was broken and twisted into a tumbled array of fragmented, mossy shards.

Clear fruits hung like orbs of glass upon the coiled branches of the larger tree, the seeds clearly visible within. *Perfectly ripe.* The Rogue Queen felt her stomach suddenly tense. It took her a moment to recognise the feeling as hunger, and her ears pricked in surprise. She hadn't even considered the need to forage.

The opportunity was here, but the clearing lay sprawled ahead of her. The Rogue Queen was hesitant.

Long, pointed ears shivered. Her nostrils flared to the scent of stone and rotting leaves. The faint sweet juices of a fruit that had splattered on the stone.

…And something else, too.

The Queen's eyes slitted. Her ears folded back against her neck, spines quivering upright. A fleeting flash of red boiled across her scales, hastily quelled. She cast a longing glance at the clear fruits, and then appeared to make a decision. Carefully neutral, she slipped back under the arched root and onto the forest floor. Hidden safely among the ferns where she could allow red to tinge her scales, she sniffed once more.

Then, she lowered her head and pattered into the undergrowth towards the battling trees.

She skirted around the broken terrain, and made her way over an upturned boulder, sticky pads clinging easily to the stone. Her scales passed from violet to the grey-green of death, patterns flitting across her as she skirted the lichens. She adjusted the tint of her base colour to mimic the light falling upon her.

She disappeared into the crack formed by a vast tree root, and reappeared at the base of the smaller tree, sniffing the air.

Her tail twitching, she pattered up the trunk and crossed a branch. Exposed to the open sky, her heart beat hard inside her and she broke into a sinewy, loping run before finally disappearing among the leaves. There, she finally relaxed. She hopped up onto a taller branch and weaved between a spray of glowing flowers until she reached a vast fruit.

Flashing yellow happiness and clouds of luminous joy, the Rogue Queen ate like she'd never ate before. The fruit was delightfully bitter and powerfully acidic; delicious, and fresh! She wasn't certain when she'd get the chance to eat again, so she stuffed her narrow body until she feared her tiny legs could no longer carry her weight.

She ate her way to the centre of the orb, to the star-shaped spray of seeds that seemed to hang within. She tucked two into her cheeks, licked her sticky paws and cleaned her face with a few quick swipes. Then she froze, nose twitching. Her ears flattening, quills shuddering, she looked up.

A figure crouched on the branch above her, simply watching with wide violet eyes. Greenish clouds and patterns of jagged orange passed over its body.

It was like her, almost; although its body was shorter, and barbed tail thicker and more powerful, its legs longer. Its crest of quills was a little less impressive. This was a creature made for fighting and fleeing, and being out in the open air.

The Rogue Queen drew her body back like a snake, quills rattling. She hissed.

The stranger lounged, seemingly unperturbed by her impoliteness.

Perched among the flowers, it was blocking her means of escape.

Patterns flitted across the stranger's body. Big patterns, and slow. *What's this Majesty doing out here, so far from her doting Hive?*

The Rogue Queen flashed indignantly red. Jagged patterns stormed across her, edged with a mocking shade of blue. *What's a Nameless Forager doing so far into a territory not his own?*

A flash of red, blue, and then green crept over him. After a moment, only the red remained. When he signalled again, his patterns were smaller, and quicker. He had the grace to lower his ears, looking slightly ashamed. *Doing my job.* The green bloomed a shade brighter. *You hunt-speak?*

Of course I hunt-speak.

Why?

To her, it was obvious. She spoke with her spines raised and chest puffed out. *I wanted to talk to foragers like you.*

Like me?

You know about the Outside.

Why would a Queen ever want to know about the Outside? The hive has everything you could ever need.

The Queen hissed again. Ordinarily, sounding was very, very impolite. And she had done it twice. *To forage. To run. To jump. To smell. To see.* She paused. *...To be free.*

Suddenly the Nameless Forager's green colouration disappeared, replaced by creeping clouds of red and white. *Rogue Queen. You are a Rogue Queen.* After a moment, his patterns swelled into pure crimson. *Why would you want to leave, Rogue Queen? Did you not have enough luxury in your life?*

The Rogue Queen's quills rattled warningly. *There is no luxury in captivity. Have you ever seen your Queen flash happiness? Ever seen them glow?* she paused. *Have you ever seen them at all?*

The Nameless forager's quills stiffened, and he billowed orange at the implications.

You wouldn't be the only one. The rogue queen arched in teal triumph, ears out and spines lying flat.

Her branch trembled as the Nameless Forager dropped down, facing her. He was stockier than she was, with longer legs. Her shoulders stood low to the ground. But her long, curving neck brought them nose to nose.

You know nothing of life Outside, he flashed. *Of the struggle to find food in the Cold, Dry cycles.*

The Rogue Queen admired the redness of his rage and the fact that he somehow resisted the urge to hiss at her.

She countered the intensity of his reds with her own, flickering with fiery orange. *No,* she admitted. *But I will.*

*What about the struggle of trying to keep **your** bellies full while the Nameless slowly starve?*

Don't feed me your righteous anger! she noticed that the forager had begun to sway and mirrored the movement. *Try starving your Queen and see what happens to the Hive!*

They wouldn't last a second. You won't last a second! You'll go crawling back to your workers and drones the second night falls!

Try me, Forager! I'm never going back. She danced up to him, sidling on the curved tree branch as she waved her barb. Angry flowers bloomed across her body. *I'd rather starve in freedom than rot among their Majesties forever!*

Just you wait!

He switched, mirroring her, and arched his back. They were nose to nose when the Rogue Queen raised her quills and flared her nostrils. She gave a chattering trill, then twisted around and showed him the colourless underside of her tail.

The Rogue Queen had just declared war.

The Nameless Forager arched in rage and sprang back. Twittering, the Queen disappeared beneath her branch and dropped among the tree roots. She followed a winding path and disappeared into a crack in the earth, springing back into view among the ferns. He followed her in close pursuit, ferns springing away from them, scales flashing bright among the leaves.

Out in the open, under the soaring roots, they goaded one another with elaborate colours.

When the Valis' colourful language wasn't enough, there was the war-dance; an expression of pure, raw emotion. The dance served as explanation, as argument, and for some, the perfect opportunity to show off.

There were no words, only an explosion of emotion and vibrancy.

Under the delicate curve of an arching root they paced in a tight circle, bodies indistinguishable from one another, joined by the art that rippled over their skin. Neon colours tossed self-preservation to the sidelines; if either was spotted by a predator here, then nature herself would decide a winner.

Orange, yellow, blue, red. There was no meaning to the Forager's patterns, other than a show of control. With a sudden jerk he leaped upwards, turning over himself in a sharp, spine-bending pirouette.

The Queen's skin swirled in elaborate challenges, and she sprang up. She mirrored his leap, spinning in an elegant ballet, tail over head.

They landed tail to nose, switched places, and then leaped again. As she passed him, the length of her body twisted into intricate shapes which he couldn't possibly mirror, her scales spinning reverse kaleidoscopes. When he began to descend, she latched onto the arching root and chittered rudely down at him.

Mine was higher.

A rainbow of red and orange bloomed from the Forager's head to his tail. And then, he simply disappeared, melting into the ferns as his scales turned perfectly reflective.

The Rogue Queen panicked. Her body was long and elegant and capable of the most elaborate turns and leaps. Her camouflage skills were improving, but some of the humble foragers' tricks were still beyond her. As the ferns unfurled their leaves to cover the spot where he had disappeared, her heart beat faster. She whisked up onto the top of the arching root and frantically looked around for something to use, gazing up at the bright flowers and neon lights.

…And there she froze, hypnotised by the flora she had longed to see for so long.

The Queen closed her eyes and remembered. The bustling emptiness of the Hive shone clear in her mind. She thought of everything she loved and longed for in a stark contrast to the world she had left behind.

The Rogue Queen couldn't hide; so she made herself as bright as she possibly could. Into her skin she poured years of dreams, thoughts and memories. She recreated the images that haunted her while lying awake, grey with hopeless emptiness.

Neon colours flowed across her, bursting into fluorescent being; neon pinks and greens and oranges and yellows. The colours of hope and joy and wonder; and those of triumph and longing. The shapes bled into one another at first, then quickly sharpened. Unhurried, the colours faded and mottled and grew. Bright fades and highlights formed. She transformed her body into a living bouquet of flowers that she had yet to see.

The Rogue Queen swayed for a moment longer, trying to mimic the faintest breeze stirring the treetops, and for that moment the flowers lived and breathed.

She opened her eyes and caught a flicker of movement.

The Nameless Forager slowly slid into being before her. They swayed at one another, cautiously pacing in a tight circle, but both knew that the dance was coming to an end.

They looked at one another, and finally faced one another, chest to chest, bodies arched. They sniffed each other's noses. It was as though they were each greeting an old friend.

Rogue Queen, the forager said, with a tinge of lavender.

She bowed her head, ears lowered. *Forager.*

There was a moment of stillness, in which the trees whispered and no life flickered across their scales. A faint drizzle of rain began to swirl through cracks in the canopy, shimmering in shafts of light.

Then the Forager brightened into plain, monotone grey. His patterns were simple and plain. *The Outside makes you happy.*

The Queen slowly settled back on her haunches. *You're as angry with your life as I was,* she signalled. She hesitated for a moment, growing dull.

I didn't think the Queens had a reason to be angry. The Forager said. He paused. *I never asked why. Will you tell me?*

The Queen hesitated. *I was trapped. Lonely,* she said, her body slowly consumed by a creeping cloud of blue. *The Foragers and Soldiers of the Valis Hives have many words. The Queens are taught only three; 'hunger', 'sleep' and 'dirt'. I had nothing to look forward to but making more bitter creatures like you.*

He flashed bright orange. *I'm not bitter.*

Be that as it may. Is anyone really happy, in the hive?

For a moment, the Forager did not answer. *I've seen happiness,* he said. *Yellow flashes and fluorescence. Not enough.*

The Rogue Queen gleamed a dull affirmation.

A long, grey moment passed. Then the Forager raised his head. *Change is needed,* he flickered. Then he looked at her.

I can't go back. The Queen closed her eyes. *All I want is this. To be free.*

She imagined the hive dragging her back into its warmest, cosiest corner. Tightening the guards. The foragers warned to dull their skin and keep their emotions safe and tight. The piercingly lonely routine of eat, be tended, and sleep.

Her scales clouded to a dull, stormy grey. Her patterns formed a stark red contrast.

I'm only a Queen, she looked away across the clearing. *Even if I wanted to make change, they'd avert their eyes.*

She heard the Forager's paws scuff the root. He settled down beside her, and she was surprised by his warm, lavender tone. *Then go,* he said. *Be free.*

She looked up, green gratitude sweeping over her. *And you?* A flutter of hopeful blue crept up her back, but she formed no words.

He looked back at her, a faint rose blush tinging his silhouette. *Maybe.* He faded away into a deep, longing indigo, then black. *To form a new hive?*

No, the Rogue queen's spines trembled. *For now, just to be together.*

To her surprise, the Forager faded back to grey. *Not many rogues survive.*

It would be a risk, she acknowledged.

The Forager hesitated. *I... can't come with you. But...* He seemed to come to a decision. *I'll go back home. I'll be a bridge. And maybe one day, things will change. Maybe then, you can come back to us.*

I'm not even from your hive, the Queen said cautiously.

He nosed at her neck, ripples of yellow spreading out from the point of contact. *Someday, that won't matter.*

Clouds of blue and luminous yellow flourished across the Rogue Queen's back. Her quills dropped, ears lowered. Together they looked away towards the fruit tree, watching a single violet leaf spiral down to the forest floor.

By the time the Queen glanced back, the Forager was gone.

She stayed for a while longer, taking in the stranger's scent while it still lingered.

Someday...

But in the meantime, she had *this*.

There was no reason for sadness. She had places to go and people to meet, dances to be danced and an entire rainbow to explore. A vibrant pulse of excitement ran from her nose to the tip of her tail, and she plunged down into the ferns, leaving the clearing behind.

She bounded away into her chaotic forest world, ever-changing. At the border of the Hive's boundary, she paused atop a rise and removed the seeds from her mouth. She pressed them into a worn-down hollow in the rock, filled with moist leaves and decaying foliage. Then she crossed into the true unknown.

Beyond lay a new world. New sights, new smells, new friends.

Before even leaving the vicinity of the Hive, she had seen so much, and there was so much more to explore. Her heart sang, her colours joyous, as she sprang up over rocks that felt like mountains and leapt between the branches of titanic trees. She rested below the tree canopy, gathering soft flowers and leaves into the crotch of a tree and looking out from her makeshift nest.

There, she watched the flowers dance as the wind picked up, and the faint shimmer of rain become crashing waterfalls as the drizzle became a deluge. Thunder cracked high above the forest, and she was torn between wonder and fear of what might have caused such a terrible roar.

One by one, the ferns furled back into buds, and the entire forest transformed.

Streams began to form on the forest floor, silver threads and foaming rapids winding along a network of ravines. The rain washed away her trail. It was as if she'd stepped into a whole new world, washing her paws clean of the Queen that had once been.

Filled with joy, she gazed up past the canopy and

admired the shafts of watery light, the cascades pouring from the tree canopy. She squeaked out loud as there was a flash of white light from somewhere beyond the trees, brighter than anything she'd ever known. It fragmented the spray into rainbows, before fading away. Dazed and thrilled, she felt the curiosity spark a fire in her chest.

The Rogue Queen's two favourite things were those that were strange, and those that were new.

She left the safety and warmth of her nest and whisked away towards the light.

Even then, the Rogue Queen knew that she'd never look back.

Child of the Mountain

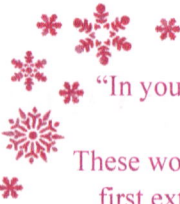

"In your tongue, we are Mountain-dwellers."

These words were said long ago by the first extra-terrestrial companion of Rifthopper Bailey Jones. He remembers them as if they were spoken yesterday, despite Seven-horn being long, long gone.

So imagine Bailey's surprise when he opens up an ancient journal and finds the face of his dear friend staring back at him. Over weeks and months, Bailey translated the journal into his own native tongue; and found the life story of a Mountain-dweller, written exactly as it was spoken. Finally, Bailey was able to hear the voice of his friend once again, and in the process learn more about the Mountain-dwellers than anyone had before.

So, here is Bailey's translation; and the story of a life in the Mountain-heart.

Map of the Mountain-Heart

I was the only one born in my winter. Though my sight was still blurry, I remember it all with perfect clarity.

I slid out into the cold through a soft, gelatinous membrane onto a carpet covered in wiry hairs. Enormous paw pads lay folded underneath my body. At first I was lead-heavy, hardly moving. I looked around with bleary eyes, and saw blue, glossy pods lying affixed, jewel like, to the faintly warm ground. I would later come to recognise them as my kin – unborn Mountain-Dwellers like I was mere moments ago. They lay still and dormant, tucked away from the sheer cold that pooled around my muzzle.

Beyond those, the world was blurry.

I was alone, the cold seeping through my fur and to my bones. I tilted a floppy ear to the burble of something that one day, I would understand as voices.

The sound stirred me into motion. Without truly knowing why, I tilted back my head and let out a bleating, keening wail into the dark.

***

Eight-horn Watcher told me that it hesitated before entering the nursery, hardly daring to believe what could be clearly heard.

The nursery room was dark – darker than any other room in the village. It was lit only by threads of light that broke through the icy walls – mostly covered by threadbare hide that bore the stiffness of centuries and struggled to keep out the cold. Still, Eight-horn's second eyes deciphered the faintest glints, and it carefully followed the sound of my voice, picking the way through a maze of dormant eggs.

I was lying in an ancient and dilapidated corner, where slick ice shone through the frayed edges of the hide cover. The walls here were jagged from repeated expansions, and the warmth had slowly fallen away. Ears spread and tail twitching in bewilderment, Eight-horn drifted slowly into my view as it bent down to see me.

The Watcher's ears flicked up, and it stepped forward, blinking slowly.

Covered in blueish liquid and shivering in the cold, I must have been a pitiable sight. I was afraid, helpless in this new and hostile world.

I bleated once more, my voice ringing sharply against the ice.

Still Eight-horn stood, frozen in horror.

My kind can only emerge in the conditions they were laid, and our pods can lie dormant sometimes for hundreds of moon-turns. My winter was the coldest season the elders had ever known, and no new life was expected.

Eight-horn looked at my egg sac, tucked away into the coldest and oldest part of the nursery.

And though it never told me, the Nursery-Watcher would have known then that I had no living life-givers, no family.

So it would have to make the choice for me.

As I let out another pitiful cry, Eight-horn stepped forward, taking my tiny weight into a warm and furry chest. Eight-horn looked at me, and I looked back, best I could.

In this bitter year, most of the adults were busy teaching and training last year's new-horns. There had been many of them last year, during a mid-cold and plentiful season, and all efforts had been put towards ensuring their survival. I was unlikely to last, and there were few skilled parents who would be ready for the challenge. The nursery-watcher hadn't even been ready.

Letting out a small, cold breath, Eight-horn stood, and cautiously picked its way out of the nursery room. Tail quivering in the slightest anticipation, it set out for the hollow of the Chief.

***

Soon after, I stared up at a ceiling made of clear ice, hypnotised by its slick, rainbowy shine and the bone supports within. Now that I was clean and dry, my fur was a delicate pink, with white speckles across the belly and nose; the perfect imitation of a light snow shower. Already I had the beginnings of a mane between my ears. The air was still cold but held tightly to the chest of the Nursery watcher, I was no longer shivering.

I did not understand the commotion going on around me, and wouldn't for many moon-turns. I listened anyway, ears pricked, and nostrils flaring.

"Mountain's Mercy! Why would you bring it here?"

"I had to," Eight-horn's low bleat was soothingly familiar, but quietly monotone. "Didn't have anywhere else."

"Have you spoken to Chief Many-horn?" one voice said.

"Yes. The Chief took it as a sign of hope – that even in this bitter cold, new life can emerge."

"Emerging is all well. But now we have to keep it that way!" The speaker paused. "It's hard enough keeping the three of us alive this year."

Another Mountain-dweller looked up from where it was tending to a bubbling black broth. The smell that emerged from it was spicy and rich, and set my nose twitching. A dark peach, this one had no horns to speak of. "Five-horn Forager is right," it said hesitantly. "There must be someone else?"

"The experienced are training the new-horns that emerged last winter! The rest refused. As Nursery watcher, I cannot let it die."

Five-horn Forager spoke again. "I haven't even given life yet – none of us have, especially Fire-keeper! We're not ready."

Fire-keeper shot an accusatory glance, lion-like mane stiffening. The two's gazes met for a fleeting moment before Five-horn finally turned away, ears lowered.

As though nothing had happened, Fire-keeper placed aside a stained stirring-stick and slowly stood. "What about its life-giver? It cannot refuse."

"This one has lain dormant for as long as I've been Watcher. For as long as my mentor was a Watcher, and its mentor. Its life-givers have long gone."

"We are not guardians, Eight-horn. We've hardly passed our first solstice." Five-horn Forager's voice trailed off into a low bleat, but it sounded resigned.

I yawned widely, watching the speaker with half-lidded eyes. I listened to the soft clatter of the ivory shards tied around its neck.

Eight-horn shifted me into a more comfortable position, causing me to squeak. When it spoke, its voice was small. "We have no other choice." It looked down at me. "In any case, our duty might not last for very long."

The Forager said nothing, nostrils flaring briefly.

Fire-keeper slowly came to take a closer look, watching in amazement. "It's so small," it said. "It won't take much feeding."

It and Five-Horn Forager exchanged another glance.

"Cooking meals *is* Fire-keeper's job," the Nursery-watcher said hopefully.

Five-horn Forager shook its ears. "But *getting* them is mine!" it grumbled. With a faint burble, the forager tied a pouch to its belly, picked up a spear, and disappeared out into the corridor beyond.

As soon as it was gone, Fire-keeper and Eight-horn visibly relaxed. They looked at one another, and then Fire-keeper held out its broad pad-hands. Eight-horn placed me into them.

Cradled by a warm, sweet-scented new presence, I fell asleep.

***

Fire-keeper and Eight-Horn's first three moonrises were easy. I slept so much that they kept thinking I was dead. Fire-keeper woke me on the next, afraid that their duty was over before it had even begun.

I kept them awake for the next four with wailing bleats as I grew with alarming speed.

After being fed a thick and heavy broth, I was once again lost to the world.

Until now, life for the three Mountain-dwellers had

plodded along with agonizing slowness. They did their respective duties and kept village life moving mechanically along. Fire-Keeper still tended its own; disappearing for long periods out into the village. When it returned to my incessant wailing, it wished out loud that the chaos would just stop.

Eight-horn Watcher tended its duty resolutely. "Don't say that here. The little one will understand one day," it scolded gently.

"If it survives," Fire-keeper said softly. But from that point on, it cared without complaint.

Five-Horn Forager did not return until those first dreadful days were over.

The delicacies it brought back were worth it, though.

It wasn't long before I could stand, and my guardians' worst fears were realised. From day one, my defining personality trait was curiosity, so I was going to be even more trouble than they thought. I kept lunging for the fire, or trying to scamper out into the village. For once, the Nursery-watcher's four eyes weren't enough.

When I could walk on two feet, Fire-Keeper let me stumble beside as it walked a winding path. It carefully wound leaves soaked in oil to bone torches along each of the hallways and re-lit them. Fire-Keeping was a long and tedious daily task, but one that was carried out without regret. Its route finished by making sure that the ritual fires in the main hall and common rooms remained warm, lit, and inviting.

Today's journey seemed less arduous than usual, though. Fire-keeper watched me with amusement in the tilt of its ears.

In my first stumbling steps, I tripped over huge paw pads as I spun to stare in fascination at the shimmering hallways beyond the boundary of my hearth-hollow.

Fire-keeper watched, eyes shining in the torchlight.

When the air grew colder nearer the surface I began to shiver, so Fire-keeper picked up and carried me the rest of the way.

I tried to touch a bone support that was beginning to

protrude from a cavern wall as the ice melted over ages of torchlight.

"The Mountain Heart is made from the carcasses of Mountain-crawlers," Fire-keeper rumbled. It held me up so that I could see more long, curved bones within the clear ice. "Long ago, they hid in this mountain from a terrible blizzard and were buried. They rotted away, leaving these caves for our village, and their bones as support."

I reached out, brushed the tips of my pads along that same wall, and then drew back from the chill with a displeased little bleat.

"Cold? Yes, the Mountain is a cruel mistress. But she is merciful, too."

Our progress drew glances in the busier tunnels, and the crowd parted around us as we stepped into the central chamber and renewed its blaze. Fire-keeper's ears lowered. Even at the time, I sensed that something was wrong.

When the bitter winter began to draw to an end, I began to show my first signs of horns – little nubs forming beneath the fur either side of my ruff.

Excitedly, Eight-horn began to tie leftover scraps of leather and wiry hide together. I whimpered and itched at my forehead even as Eight-horn carefully worked on a necklace made from small and colourful beads.

Finally the points burst through, and my forelock was stained with the blue blood of my first tiny crown. Eight-horn's ears rose with joy and, before the blood dried, draped me in a heavy little shawl made from mountain-crawler hide.

I was still too small to withstand the cold.

My three guardians helped me up through a long, icy labyrinth of tunnels and through a corridor of stone. Finally, the rocky walls peeled away to a world of white.

I shut my eyes against the brightness, but it seethed in my second pair. Finally, I opened them.

I looked out over a world of vastness and wonder. The mountainside swept away below me, piercingly white, before fading into a shroud of choking fog far below. I gazed in awe at the huge red sun that hung above the distant peaks and bathed the snow in rose. I looked, wide-eyed, up to the two great moons in the sky, and the mountain-crawlers trundle across the distant slopes, wormlike bodies crinkling as they moved on heavy legs. Overwhelmed, I took my first step out into the light.

I disappeared immediately into a deep snowdrift.

At the sharp touch of frozen water, I scrambled back in a burst of flakes, hurrying away from the sensation that would soon be all too familiar.

I bleated in panic as the cold clung, and Eight-horn smiled and took me to its chest, eyes sparkling in warmth and triumph.

Unbeknownst to me, with my first step out onto the mountainside, I had just earned my first name; New-horn.

***

My first words arrived shortly after my first horns. In sharp, clipped little bleats I first began to call for comfort, and for food.

My first question was merely a signal; I patted the sharp little nubs between my ears, and then the bare forelock of Fire-keeper's. I knew that there was a difference, but didn't understand why.

"...Will grow, soon," I said, croakily repeating my lifegivers.

Fire-Keeper shook its ears and did not elaborate.

Eight-horn Watcher shed another set of horns. The Mountain-dweller lost its name, and for a time was treated with cautious sympathy. It rarely spoke, posture sullen. I watched in fascination as those horns gradually regrew, before my guardian finally declared a new name.

Nine-horn Watcher took it all in stride.

The days warmed, the snow receded, and rivers flooded down the mountainside. There were times when only the tallest drifts remained. The rocky peaks began to emerge, and snowmelt plunged down into the mist that rose ever higher from the valleys below. I began to see more of the world, although I didn't understand why I was being shown it, at first.

First Nine-horn took me to meet the Mountain-crawlers and their keepers on the mountainside, where I stood in awe watching the great, ten-legged beasts. They trundled along without a care, scooping up entire chambers worth of snow with whiskery tendrils. They left vast rifts behind them that left the rocky mountainside exposed. A sprinkling of powder-snow shimmered on the air around the herd, lightly dusting the flanks of the massive beasts and settling on the first strands of my mane.

"These are the creatures that made our home," I said to Nine-horn in awe.

Nine-horn's ears twitched acknowledgement. "The Keepers here look after them."

Some Keepers perched atop the Mountain-crawlers' backs, teasing clots of snow from their fur. Others scurried around the great creatures' legs, preventing them from freezing to the ground if ever they paused. More still made sure that their whiskers kept clean and healthy, and that the other end remained unblocked by rocks, stones and weeds.

"They eat snow?" I asked one of the Keepers, from a rocky outcropping above the deep snowdrifts.

The Keeper smiled. It stood on the surface of the snow on broad, padded feet, leaving barely a track. I still had not mastered the art. "They eat what's in the snow."

"Water?"

"Little things. Little alive things."

I shivered, and looked towards Nine-Horn Watcher.

"Not like us," the Keeper chuckled, as though knowing.

"How can something like this need to be taken care of?" I asked, watching the huge creatures in awe.

The Keeper tipped its head, blinking slowly. "They don't always," it said. "There are herds out there without Keepers, but all life on the Mountain is fragile. We just help make it less so."

On the way back, Nine-horn showed me the nursery

chamber where jewel-like eggs still lay dormant, blue and shimmering and softly pulsating. "This is where you came from."

"I was once... like this?" I looked around in amazement, as vague feelings and blurry memories flooded back. "What will happen to all of them?"

"I'll take care of them, and watch them, and make sure that the nursery is stable. Then, when they are ready, they emerge. I or another nursery-watcher will bring them to their life-giver."

I paused, tilting an ear. "I was your mountain-crawler," I said with sudden understanding and amazement.

Nine-horn rumbled in amusement. "I suppose you are."

"Why are you showing me?"

"As a New-horn you need to learn how the Village works. And one day, you'll need to decide your place in it."

My tail and ears quivered nervously. "What if I don't want to?" I said. "I'm happy here, learning with you."

"Oh, New-Horn. You have plenty of time. This Solstice, last winter's new-horns will choose. You have a whole winter until yours!"

I let out a small breath. "Is that a long time?"

Nine-horn hesitated, and then spoke. "Yes, small one. It's a very, very long time."

***

When the shadows lengthened and the days grew longer, the horns atop my head grew too, into tightly curved spirals. When running a pad across them, they were rough to the touch. And as the great flakes became a fine sprinkle of powdery summer snow, they began to itch dreadfully. Only pressing my skull into an icy wall would numb the pain. As each day passed, the pain worsened. Finally as I shoved them into the hard, cold surface of the cavern wall, there was a dreadful snap.

I jerked back in shock, and my shed horn clattered to the ground. I stared down in amazement and slight horror. I felt briefly elated, overjoyed even. I was growing – becoming more experienced, and the first horn-shedding was an event to be celebrated. Even more than that, I had survived the most difficult time of a Mountain-dweller's life!

Happiness was quickly followed by a fleeting feeling of terror.

I knew that shedding horns changed things; that Nine-Horn's life had changed when its horns had shed.

So what did this mean? I did not want to change. I was happy just to be me.

When Five-horn Forager returned, carrying armfuls of edible herbs and sweet-scented flowers, I scampered and hid behind the fire plinth.

Five-Horn ignored me as it sorted out its bounty into various nooks and crannies in the icy walls, little hollows that kept them cold and dry. Tail wiggling as it worked, it finally looked towards me.

It saw four beady little eyes peeking over the fire plinth, two ears, and only one horn.

Its ears pricked, first in surprise, and then joy. "New-horn!" The forager bleated, and hurried over. "You've shed!"

I covered my face behind one pad-hand, looking up only as the horn was eased from my grasp. I clasped my paws over my chest.

Five-horn turned the horn over, examining it closely. "A good shed, for the first. Strong."

"What should I do now?"

Five-horn tilted an ear, considering. Then it beckoned me over to the fire plinth. It picked up a rock from within the ashes, raised it, and then brought it down, crushing the horn between rock and stone. Shards of ivory scattered in all directions, and I flattened my ears, staring in amazement and disappointment.

Five-horn picked through the pieces, selecting the best shards, then knelt and offered them to me.

I stared. "Wh... why did you break it?"

"These broken shards will be your most prized

possession one day. Especially if you spend time away from the village."

"…How?"

Five-horn didn't answer at first. My guardian stood and walked towards the far wall, where a few leaves were lifted from a hollow. Five-horn gestured to the broken shards around its neck. Placing the leaves into the hollow, it struck two of them together. The ivory released a shower of sparks, and the leaves burst alight into a sharp white flame.

I watched the fire burn out, entranced, and stared down at the shards Five-horn still held.

"What happens now?"

Five-horn blinked.

"Now?"

"Do I lose my name, like Nine-horn?"

Five-horn looked at me curiously. "Until your summer comes, you won't. You don't start counting your horns until you choose your place." It cast a glance towards the door. "…But now that you have your first shed, you have a lot to learn." Five-horn's eyes glittered with an odd light. "I think it's time you learned the way of the Forager."

***

Nine-horn and Fire-keeper did not agree.

They thought I was far too small to leave the Mountain's Heart on a foraging expedition, and after a long period of tail-quivering tension and low-voiced bleats that threatened to shatter into bellows at any moment, Five-horn reluctantly stood down.

I was not unhappy about this. With only one horn and the shards that were now at my disposal, I felt more than a little underdressed.

My heart ached with curiosity. I burned to see the world below. But I also knew that foraging was often deadly. My curiosity was insatiable, but the limits of my world ended at the Keepers domain. To become a forager, even to train to be one, was to make a deadly choice. The swirling fog below the Mountain felt like a trap just waiting to spring.

So training continued as it was. I helped the healers to sort their herbs, giving meaning to the odd array of icy colours and jagged shapes. I learned the basics of making poultices and closing wounds, knowledge that would be vital if I chose any sort of outdoor caste, even Keeping.

I learned the most efficient route to tend the village fires, walking with Fire-keeper on that solitary patrol. I realised then that the way the village parted around us paralleled the way it had when Nine-horn Watcher had newly shed.

"Fire-keeper?" I asked.

Fire-keeper rumbled curiously.

"Have you ever had horns?"

Fire-keeper's ears flicked my way. "No," it said. "Never."

"Why?"

Fire-keeper blinked slowly. "I... never found an answer," it said, after a long pause. "This is just how it is."

"But you still survived," I said.

Fire-keeper nodded. "The village uses horns as tools. I don't have any of my own. Eight-horn Watcher and Five-Horn forager help best they can, but they can only do so much."

I looked away. "It's as though you've only just shed your horns. Forever."

Fire-keeper took a moment to consider, tilting one ear up. "That is true," it rumbled. "But at least I'm not alone. Your other guardians treat me just the same."

We kept on wandering, along pathways carpeted with thick pink fur, and hallways shimmering with rainbows of ice. Fire-keeper stretched up to wrap a torch in a long, vine-like leaf, and let me light the flame with my shards.

After a while, Fire-keeper spoke. "I am grateful to you, New-horn."

I was surprised, and after a moment, softly bleated "why?"

Fire-Keeper's ears flicked. "No-one has ever asked me that before. They only know that this is how I am."

I wriggled my ears slightly, but lowered my muzzle, lost in thought. Still we wandered on, through a labyrinth of tunnels, our sides close to touching, while the rest of the Mountain's Heart avoided us with lowered eyes.

Time moved on, the days lengthening. When I helped the Keepers out on the slopes, I watched the moons growing vast in the sky.

Until one day darkness fell, and I looked up from where I crouched among the rocks, pulling thorny plants from hidden water channels. My eyes widened in amazement as a great shadow swept up the mountainside. The moons were taking great chunks out of the Sun as they passed it. My second eyes strained against the brightness, yet I could not look away.

Midsummer had arrived, and with it came the solstice. Every few moon-turns, the sun was eclipsed just a little more, bathing the snow a rich-wine red.

The new-horns that came before me were soon ushered out onto the mountainside with their teachers, guardians, and life-givers. Fire-Keeper, Nine-horn Watcher and Five-horn forager brought me too, and we quietly watched as the twelve young Mountain-dwellers were arranged in a circle. The time had come for the Ceremony of the Solstice; when each New-horn would choose their place in the village. Some wore beads or had plaited their newly-grown manes into elaborate braids. Some carried spears, or pouches of clattering ivory.

Chief Many-horn stood before them, wearing a necklace of horns shed by its predecessors. The New-horns hardly dared to burble among themselves, and tails were lowered, quivering with nerves.

I was almost as nervous. I knew that when my time came, I would go through this alone.

Chief stood tall, and with a tilt of the head signalled a New-horn to step forward.

The New-horn's ears were flat, mane stiff. Its nostrils flared as Chief Many-horn spoke.

"Young one. You have trained hard, but do you feel that you are ready to take your place in the Mountain's Heart as a Mountain-dweller?"

"Yes," the young one said, in a tiny voice. "I have shed four of my horns. I am experienced enough. I am ready." It stood just a little bit taller, its voice growing louder as its confidence built. "From this moon-turn, I declare myself First-horn Keeper."

It bowed its head, tilting its ears up.

"Welcome, First-Horn Keeper, to our tribe."

First-horn Keeper stepped aside, and went to join its life-giver, away from the waiting New-horns.

Chief Many-horn repeated this question again for the next, and the next, and the next. Some of the New-horns leapt into their declarations. Others were more hesitant, lingering on their decision with more caution.

By the time the last new-horn stepped forth, there were three new Keepers, two new Traders, two new Healers, two Foragers, and a Watcher. Nine-horn Watcher's ears pricked with surprise and glee at the realisation, for the first time, of who would become its apprentice and successor.

With every choice made, I thought about how I'd feel. I tried to imagine spending the rest of my life living with that choice.

…And my mane began to prickle with unease.

The final New-horn stepped forward.

"From this moon-turn, I declare myself First-horn Defender."

My ears went up. I looked towards my Guardians, to find that they were blinking too.

"I've never met a Defender before," I rumbled to Nine-horn beside me.

Nine-horn Watcher hesitated before replying, voice hushed. "That's because there are none. Not until now."

My ears pricked. "Why now?"

"This New-Horn must have felt that it was needed."

"Will First-Horn Defender need to teach this role to me?"

81

"No. As the first Defender for three generations, it must teach itself first."

I found my mind spinning at the idea of choosing a role that did not exist. Suddenly my choice felt even heavier. "Are there others?"

"Other what?"

"Roles that I cannot be taught?"

Nine-horn watcher flicked its ears in affirmation but turned its attention back towards Chief Many-horn as the ceremony was drawn to a close.

When it was over, a sprinkling of summer snow began to fall. The mountain-dwellers scattered across the mountainside to tend their respective duties. It was as though nothing had changed. Each First-horn had chosen their place, and each one would be happy. Each became a small piece of the rhythm that kept the Mountain's Heart alive.

And it would be my turn next.

***

I grew until I was as tall as my guardians, and my training persisted. At first I struggled to stay above the snow, until one day I went out to meet the Keepers and realised that I had not left a single track behind me. I spent a lot of time with the Keepers and the Healers, their knowledge dulling the edge of that persistent hunger. I watched from the background as the traders haggled and spoke.

One day as I was settled atop the vast back of a Mountain-crawler, I felt something heavy settle on my mane.

I tilted my face towards the sky, and was surprised to find huge snowflakes swirling slowly down from a red-stained sky. The first great flakes of winter had arrived.

I now knew the ways of the keeper, the watcher, the healer, the fire-keeper. I was less experienced in the ways of the trader, which was a life of negotiation and minor conflict. The name of Chief would be off-limits for a long time yet.

My guardians decided that now was the time for me to learn the way of the Forager, before winter's chill became too deep.

They did not speak of the Defender, or any roles beyond it.

When I began to show a proficiency for healing herbs, Five-horn Forager had begun showing me those it brought back from the valley below. My guardian brought only a fraction of its bounty back to our hearth-hollow. Others went to the traders, who helped distribute them among the hearths without foragers. Others still went to the healers.

I learned that a forager needed to know the difference between healing herbs and food, and the basics of first aid in a world where there were often more deaths than births. Some of the most delicious foods closely resembled healing herbs which, although very useful, were also very toxic.

Slowly, I learned the Forager's duties, and a sense of dread began to ripple up my spine. The first great flakes were falling, and soon winter would plunge the mountain into the deepest cold of the year.

It was time for Five-Horn to take me on my first foraging trip.

I shed once more, and Five-horn Forager showed me how to use this horn, alongside hide and bone to make a spear. Making one that was sturdy as well as useful may as well have been a form of art.

With Five-horn's help, though, I managed.

Soon after, it was time to go. Five-horn tied a hide pack around my shoulder and handed me my spear as though it was rare and fragile. Although nearly fully grown, I felt small and afraid. My other two guardians gathered to see us off. They bowed their heads in silent warmth, and Nine-horn Watcher rested its pads upon my cheeks, looking into my four eyes.

There weren't many words to be said.

Finally, Nine-horn lowered its pads.

I looked towards Fire-keeper.

"Walk light. Run fast. Keep safe," Fire-keeper rumbled, looking from Five-Horn Forager to myself in turn. "Come home to us."

Five-Horn forager's ears flicked. Then it turned its back, and I had no choice but to follow.

We left the village on a different path to what I was used to, descending the slopes through a tight zigzag down the cliffs. The mist rose up around us, and ice crystals began to form in the trailing tips of my mane. I shivered for the first time since the season of my birth. As we descended, the ice formed jagged shapes in the fog.

Five-horn reached out and plucked something from the cliffside. I looked closely and found a knot of creeping fungus caps that blended into the stone. I placed some into my basket.

"What is the mist?" I asked.

"Cold," Five-horn said. "Pain given shape."

As we descended, I began to realise what my mentor meant. My limbs began to grow heavy, breaths coughing. As the altitude lowered, my body suffered. The air felt thick, as though I was breathing water. But I kept plodding on, determinedly after Five-horn.

The sun shone red through banks of mist as we descended, and shadows emerged. The silence was oppressive, with low reverberations shivering from somewhere below. My ears whisked out, and I searched frantically for something beyond the silence. Finally, something loomed over us. Gnarled tendrils of ice and snow formed a gaping cavern. As we stepped into the cavernous maw, the mist cleared.

And around us, I saw life. More plants clung to the world around than I had ever seen before. What had at first seemed to be the walls of a cave turned out to be tightly knotted trunks and stems, twisting into a ceiling above us that kept the falling snow at bay.

There was more foliage than I had ever known existed – some that I recognised from our cooking pots and the healers, but many of them new. Faded pastel colours blended into deep blue shadows. Clear vines shimmered like ice, veins of dark fluid pulsing through them.

Ice crystals hanging from the tips of flowers chimed faintly as something moved in the dark.

I looked up and saw that tangles of plant life supported a ceiling of compressed snow.

We foraged, keeping to the shadows and underbrush. I picked spittleberry vines, that could clean wounds and be tossed into fires for bursts of sparks and colour. Delicious weeds sprouted from long-dead trunks, or clung to those still alive. Occasionally, I saw a bluish tendril tipped with red, dripping from holes in trees and curling around plants.

Five-horn gestured with its spear to one of the tendrils. "Parasites," it said. "Stay away from them. They burrow into flesh."

"What if they get me?" I asked in horror.

"Don't return to the village. Find a place to hide, chew fever-root and go to sleep. The pain won't last very long."

My ears quivered. Boiled down to a paste, fever-root was smeared on the forehead of the sick and helped to make them cold again. When eaten, it was deadly poisonous.

With our bags filled to the brim with healing herbs, we had only enough food to share between us. Five-horn Forager ground its teeth in chagrin. "We can't go back yet," it said. "We can't go home with nothing to eat."

I nodded silently. I uprooted a plant that could be burned and made a tiny pile upon the frozen ground. In the dark, there was no telling how long we'd been here, but in the low altitude, I tired quickly. My limbs felt leaden, my heart raced, and I wasn't sure if my pads were numb with cold, or something else.

Creatures rustled. Ice crystals tinkled. Something shimmered and scattered from the light as a small blue flame spat into life.

"You seem to like being out of the Mountain," Five-horn said.

I blinked my eyes open and raised my head. "This place is new – it is frightening, but beautiful." I rearranged myself heavily into a more comfortable position. "There is so much to learn."

"So you're considering the way of a Forager, then."

New-horn hesitated, picking its words carefully. "Do you... want me to?"

Five-horn rumbled. "I want you to make the right choice, not my choice."

There was a long pause. Five-horn eventually broke it.

"So," Five-horn said, as it settled by the fire. "Have you decided?"

"I... I've been trying to," I admitted. "But I..." I hesitated. "I am not ready yet."

"Why not?"

My ears fluttered curiously, and I dragged myself awake, trying to place a clear handle on feelings that were beyond my comprehension. "I..."

"Do none of them make you feel whole?"

I blew out a long breath. "That's not it," I said finally. "All of them do."

Five-horn's tail twitched in surprise. "All of them?"

"Yes."

Five-horn Forager considered this. "In the solstice we welcomed a Defender into our ranks, the first in three Generations, so you know that the Mountain-Heart has had other roles in the past. Some of these roles are no longer needed. Some of them are needed now more than ever. Have you considered choosing one of those?"

My ears flicked up in surprise. "Like what?"

"My life-giver was a Negotiator. It would settle disputes and arguments over food and hollows, back when there were more of us. And Burrowers, who dug their way through raw ice to make our village larger." Five-horn blinked, and settled back. "...And then there were the Speakers."

"Speakers?"

"Their job was to be curious, to learn, and to share what they knew." Five-horn looked out into the darkness. "To become a speaker was a hard, hard choice. You had to be every role and none of them."

"Wh... why? Why would we need a Speaker now?" My voice caught breathlessly.

"We always need a speaker. With knowledge, they can advise Chiefs and New-horns about the right choices to make. If a straggler comes in from another tribe, the Speaker will be the one to learn their tongue. If a new role is ever needed, a Speaker will find the word for it. But most of all, by knowing, learning, and being curious, they ease fears and cull superstitions."

I was silent, watching Five-horn's eyes shining in the firelight. When I spoke, my voice was small. "Why didn't Nine-horn and Fire-keeper tell me?"

Five-horn forager took a moment to consider. "...A Speaker weaves truth, and truth invites change. Perhaps that's why it's been so long since we've had one."

I struggled to find a reply.

"There is more in the Mountain's heart for you than you know, New-horn. Think carefully, and I know you will make the right choice."

But, as I gazed out into the dark, I knew that my choice had been found.

***

The solstice arrived still carrying the cool traces of an unusually warm winter.

I stood upon a mountain slope glowing rich and rosy under the sun. The Chief and I faced one another, standing eye to eye. It felt a lot less frightening with just the two of us, and the fire of anticipation burned in my veins.

If only my last shed could have grown back in time; it was a little embarrassing to stand before the Chief with only one horn.

I cast a glance over the assembled crowd; the winter's eight New-horns stood next to their Life-givers and guardians, some waist-deep in snow. Beside them, Fire-keeper stood, its pads clasped together, its dark peach standing out against the snow. And then, the newly-shed

Six-horn Forager, forelock carefully arranged across its growing points. And finally, Nine-horn Watcher, dressed in shining necklaces and shivering in pride.

The Chief tilted its head in a familiar gesture, encouraging me to step forward. I did so without a trace of fear.

"Young one. You have trained hard, but do you feel you are ready to take your place in the Mountain's Heart?"

"Yes," I said, a low and formal bleat. "I have shed five of my horns. I am experienced. I am ready." I squared my pads upon the snow. "From this moon-turn, I declare myself First-horn Speaker."

I bowed my head, tilting my ears up.

A ripple of surprise resounded through the assembled life-givers. Even my guardians exchanged a glance.

The Chief, though, did not seem moved. "We've been waiting a long time for you," it said with slight humour. "Welcome, First-Horn Speaker, to our tribe."

Elsewhen Press

delivering outstanding new talents in speculative fiction

Visit the Elsewhen Press website at elsewhen.press for the latest information on all of our titles, authors and events; to read our blog; find out where to buy our books and ebooks; or to place an order.

Sign up for the Elsewhen Press InFlight Newsletter at elsewhen.press/newsletter

How do you hold on to hope when you're being repeatedly wrenched between worlds?

College student Bailey Jones is plucked from his world by a mysterious and unpredictable force known as the Rift, which appears to move people at random from one world to another. Stranded on an alien planet, he is relieved when he meets a fellow human, the self-styled Riftmaster, who is prepared to assist him. Although curious about his new companion's real identity, Bailey hopes that, with years of experience of the Rift, this cosmic traveller can help him find a way to return to Earth. But first, as the two of them are ripped without warning from one hostile planet to another, Bailey must rely on the Riftmaster to show him how to survive.

Riftmaster, an adventure, an exploration, is concerned with loss, and letting go, while still holding onto your humanity and identity, even when life seems hopeless.

ISBN: 9781911409915 (epub, kindle) / 9781911409816 (264pp paperback)

Visit bit.ly/Riftmaster

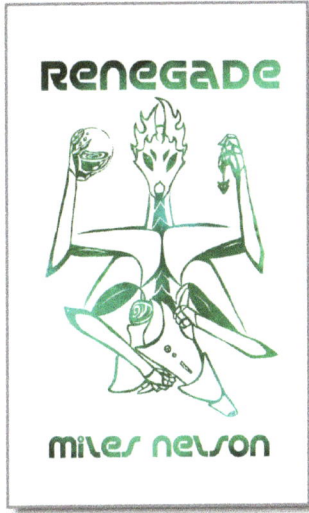

RENEGADE

MILES NELSON

The Riftmaster Ari is on their own, with nothing but their wit, their satchel, and a vow to make it back to Earth.

To do that they must stay alive, no matter the cost… but it seems that the inhabitants of this vast universe have other plans.

With Bailey gone, Ari's life should shift back to normalcy. But after discovering all that remains of their family and taking the life of their love, Ari feels more alone than ever. Their only company is the strange sickness that fights against their every move, and the starships that seem to creep across the skies of every planet they visit. Starships belonging to the Renohaiin Empire.

In their time as Riftmaster, Ari has made allies and enemies alike. Even still, the Empire's motives are hazy at the best of times, and insidious at the worst. As Ari's condition deteriorates, the Renohaiin alone might have a cure.

For now, the Riftmaster is alive. But just how far will they go to keep it that way?

Renegade is the much anticipated sequel to *Riftmaster*, the 2021 bestseller from Miles Nelson.

ISBN: 9781915304346 (epub, kindle) / 9781915304247 (320pp paperback)

Visit bit.ly/Renegade-Nelson

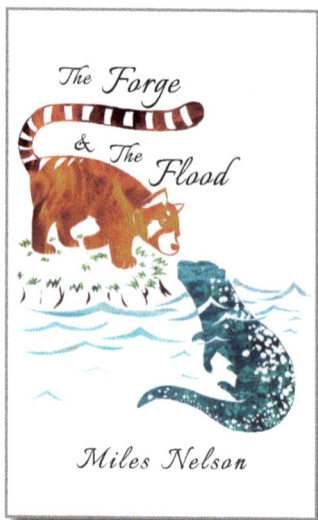

When history itself seems written to keep them apart, can two radically different peoples really find it in their hearts to get along?

Sienna is an Ailura. His kind live on the lonely island of Veramilia, bound under traditions forged by countless generations. Indigo is a Lutra. His kind goes with the flow, having lived as free as the ocean waves since the beginning of time.

When a great calamity strikes and the Ailura are forced to flee their island home, the Ailura and the Lutra come face to face for the first time in known history. In these turbulent times, it is Indigo and Sienna who are chosen to find a suitable habitat for the displaced tribe. One a princess destined to rule his kind, the other the only son of a would-be chief, the pair seem like a natural choice.

But as friendship blossoms into something more, and their journey takes them further and further from known lands, the wanderers begin to uncover secrets hidden among the ruins. Secrets which suggest the two species may not be as alien to one another as previously thought.

ISBN: 9781915304100 (epub, kindle) / 9781915304001 (184pp paperback)

Visit bit.ly/Forge&Flood

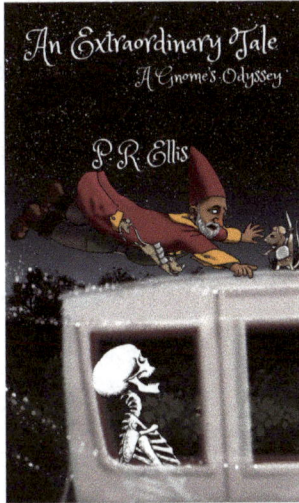

An Extraordinary Tale
A Gnome's Odyssey
P. R. Ellis

A gnome, a mouse and a skeleton meet on a train

The Fairy Queen's electrum, the most valuable material in the world, has been stolen. By chance Philbrach Hohenheim, a gnome, finds himself on the trail of the thief. A motley fellowship is formed between the gnome and other creatures. The pursuit crosses lands, times and realities until finally a major puzzle at the borders of the world is solved. On the way, Philbrach encounters giant pigeons, a sentient fungus, a seafaring merman, the Sun's chariot driver and other helps and hindrances.

ISBN: 9781915304353 (epub, kindle) / 9781915304254 (290pp paperback)

Visit bit.ly/AnExtraordinaryTale

THE MAREK SERIES BY JULIET KEMP

1   2

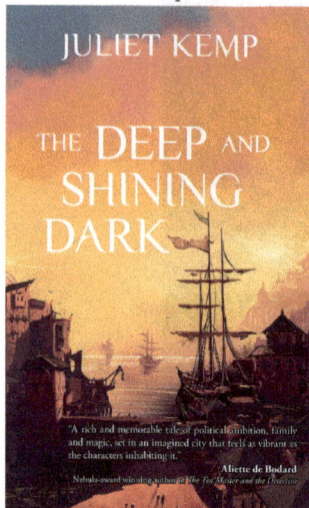

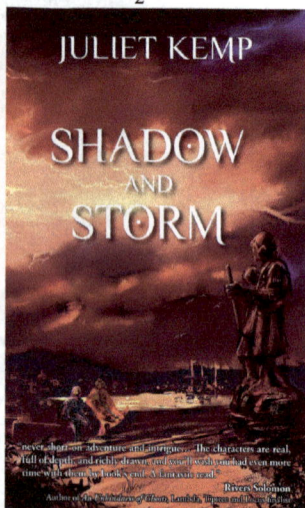

A Locus Recommended Read in 2018

"A rich and memorable tale of political ambition, family and magic, set in an imagined city that feels as vibrant as the characters inhabiting it."
Aliette de Bodard

You know something's wrong when the cityangel turns up at your door

An agreement 300 years ago, between an angel and Marek's founding fathers, protects magic and political stability within the city. A recent plague wiped out most of the city's sorcerers. Reb, one of the survivors, realises that someone has deposed the cityangel without replacing it. Marcia, Heir to House Fereno, stumbles across that same truth. But it is just one part of a much more ambitious plan to seize control of Marek. Meanwhile, city Council members connive and conspire, manipulated in a dangerous political game that threatens the peace and security of all the states around the Oval Sea. Reb, Marcia, the deposed cityangel, and Jonas, a Salina messenger, must work together to stop the impending disaster. They must discover who is behind it, and whom they can really trust.

ISBN: 9781911409342 (epub, kindle) / 9781911409243 (272pp paperback)
Visit bit.ly/DeepShiningDark

"never short on adventure and intrigue... the characters are real, full of depth, and richly drawn, and you'll wish you had even more time with them by book's end. A fantastic read."
Rivers Solomon

Never trust a demon... or a Teren politician

The new Teren Lord Lieutenant has an agenda. A young Teren magician being sought by an unleashed demon, believes their only hope may be to escape to Marek where the cityangel can keep the demon at bay. Once again Reb, Cato, Jonas and Beckett must deal with a magical problem, while Marcia tackles a serious political challenge to Marek's future.

ISBN: 9781911409595 (epub, kindle) / 9781911409496 (336pp paperback)
Visit bit.ly/ShadowAndStorm

THE MAREK SERIES BY JULIET KEMP

3   4

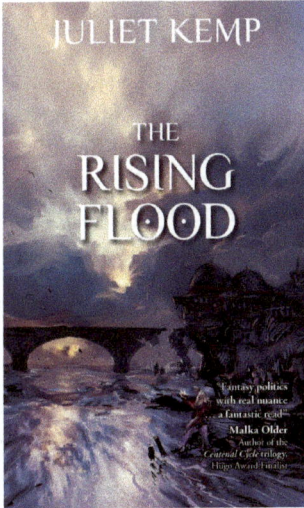 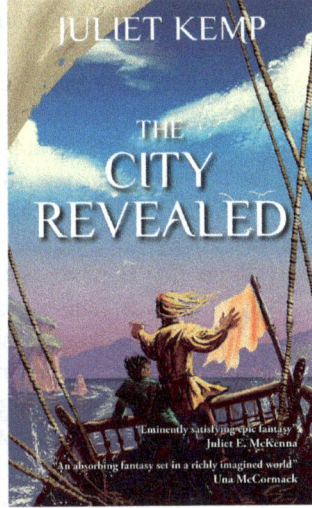

"Fantasy politics with real nuance ... a fantastic read"   **Malka Older**

Hope alone cannot withstand a rising flood

A darkness writhes in the heart of Teren, unleashing demons on dissenters. Marek's five sorcerers with the cityangel can expel a single demon, but Teren has many. Storms rampage across the Oval Sea. Menaced by the distant capital, dissension from within, and even nature itself – will the rising flood lift all boats? Or will they be capsized?

ISBN: 9781911409984 (epub, kindle) / 9781911409885 (392pp paperback)

Visit bit.ly/TheRisingFlood

"Eminently satisfying epic fantasy"   **Juliet E. McKenna**

"An absorbing fantasy set in a richly imagined world"   **Una McCormack**

Independence brings self-determination but also threats

Marek is newly-independent. Teren's expelled Lieutenant threatened to return with soldiers & war sorcerers. The common folk of Marek demand representation. Marcia, Fereno-Heir, agrees with them. She and sorcerer Reb, her lover, must convince the Council of the truth of magic, whilst her sorcerer brother, Cato, rushes to build some sort of defence.

ISBN: 9781915304315 (epub, kindle) / 9781915304216 (344pp paperback)

Visit bit.ly/TheCityRevealed

Juliet Kemp lives by the river in London, with their partners, child, dog, and too many fountain pens. They have had stories published in several anthologies and online magazines. Their employment history variously includes working as a cycle instructor, sysadmin, life model, researcher, permaculture designer, and journalist. When not writing or parenting, Juliet goes climbing, knits, reads way too much, and drinks a lot of tea.

ABOUT MILES NELSON

Miles was born and raised in the distant north, in a quaint little city called Durham.

He studied video game design at Teesside University, graduating in 2018. Since then, he has taken a step back from coding to work on his writing career, and has since led several masterclasses with New Writing North.

He has been writing all his life, and although *Riftmaster* was technically his fourth novel, he likes to pretend the first three don't exist. Whilst he is primarily a sci-fi writer who loves long journeys, strange worlds and all things space and stars, he has also had brief flings with the genres of fantasy and horror.

He often writes stories highlighting the struggles faced by the LGBTQ+ community, and tries to include themes of empathy and inclusivity in all he does. Even then, though, Miles stands firm in the belief that this is not the defining element of his stories. And although he tries to represent his community as best he can, these themes are never the main focus; because he believes that (in most cases) a person shouldn't be defined by their deviation from standard norms.

Outside of scifi and fantasy, he has a deep-rooted fascination with natural history, and collects books told from unique perspectives (be they animal, alien, or mammoths from Mars). The older, the better; his oldest book is just about to turn 100!

He currently lives in Durham City, where he runs BookWyrm, an LGBTQ+ bookshop, alongside his husband Chris.

9 781915 304490